Of Adam

A Novel by Russ Evans

PublishAmerica
Baltimore

First printing

ISBN: 1-4137-1836-1
PUBLISHED BY
PUBLISHAMERICA, LLLP.
www.publishamerica.com
Baltimore

Printed in the United States of America

In memory of Lois S. Davies,
who taught me the value of
humanity and social consciousness.

Acknowledgements

Thanks to Mike for his friendship and hours of mind-stretching conversation. It was from one of those discussions that the idea for this story sprang.

And to my friends and family who have accepted my insanity.

The voices are still there, but I'm writing them down as quickly as I can…

PROLOGUE

ADAM STOOD AT THE EDGE OF the rise overlooking the garden. His translucent skin catching the brightness of the day. Red muscles relaxed around blue veins and white cartilage. He inhaled deeply, feeling each atom of nitrogen and oxygen enter his expanding lungs. The air was sweet with blooming flowers, ripening fruit and the pungent odor of animal dung.

Cattle grazed carelessly, occasionally looking up at him and nodding in acknowledgement of his presence among them. A Bison calf skittered up the hill, stopping a hand's breadth away. Adam reached out and rubbed its thick, wooly tuft of hair as it tore the brilliant green grass from the ground. The sky was bright with midday. It was always bright. No clouds, no sun.

He knew of these things. His father had taught him about them and the universe. He had shown him the workings of the tiniest elements that made up the very grass he stood on, the history of the Earth and how to travel between the planets. Everything his father knew, he knew.

Adam walked slowly down the slope toward the gate to the garden. All of the creatures around watched him with brotherly contentment. Adam looked back. They were his companions, his co-inhabitants of this place his father called Paradise. But they were nothing more than things to rub, hold, kill and eat. They could not talk like his father. They did not feel like he did. They were not curious. They were not hungry to learn.

They had been brought to him one by one by his father. One by one they had stayed to graze and sleep. They did little else. His father told him not to complain. He would soon take care of his predicament. Soon he brought wonderful trees and fruits to eat. Vegetables appeared near his resting place and his father told him stories. He was content. He lacked for nothing.

The garden Paradise was beautiful, cool and comfortable. A stream coursed through its center sending a splash of fresh water near him as it ran around the smooth rocks that lined its glassy bottom. Adam used it only to drink from. He never bathed. He never had need to.

Some days stories came to him unbidden, untold by his father. Adam often wondered how and why this happened. He never forgot them.

His father had explained that these stories were his gift to him and, as he discovered more and more stories, he would give them to him in this way. He would never forget them as long as he lived. His father had also promised that that would be for a long time; a long time.

Yet, in his world, a world made just for him, Adam was lonely.

Again his father promised a solution to his loneliness. Soon, he said, there would be someone much like him, someone who could talk to him, who would share Paradise with him.

The bright blue sky began to darken. It was time to sleep. Adam walked through the garden to his place of rest.

He stopped next to the apple tree and looked at the red, ripe fruit, snatched one, ate, and let his thoughts wander, as he did every evening before sleep. Maybe a story would come tonight, he hoped.

Brightness filled the tiny niche behind the maples that made up his resting place. Adam felt his heart leap with joy as the shimmering figure of his father stepped out from behind the largest tree. His "coat," his father called it, hung loosely to the ground. It was brilliant white. Whiter than anything Adam had ever seen. Beneath the coat were the usual dark blue coverings called "clothes." Adam felt strange every time he saw his father. He did not wear coverings like him. There was no need for clothing here in Paradise.

The blurred face of his father refused to give up details. Adam could almost see the hint of a nose and eyes that were possibly blue, a diffused mop of bright reddish yellow hair on top of his head, but no details. It was always as if his father was not really there.

That is, until he talked. Then Adam was filled with warmth and love for the one who had given him all of this Paradise.

"Adam?" his father called.

"Here, Father. In my resting place."

The glowing figure moved over next to him. "As I suspected. How are you today?"

"I am fine. I am always fine, Father. You know that, but you ask anyway. Why?"

"Habit, I guess."

"Is my newest companion ready to join me?"

"Nearly." His father moved the fuzzy image of hands behind his radiant coat. "There is a problem."

"In Paradise? Father, I know your sense of humor. This is not a funny joke."

"No. No. It is no joke. I am ninety-eight percent complete, but I've run into a snag. I wanted to tell you there would be a long delay before your companion is ready."

Adam felt disappointment well up within his chest. It was a feeling he was not used to. He choked back tears. "I-I will be content. Send me more stories until my companion is ready."

"I'm afraid that won't be possible either." The vague face showed dark lines around the eye spots. Was his father also feeling the anguish?

"Why not, Father? Have I done something that is not good?"

"No. You are always good, Adam. You don't know how to act otherwise. Bad is a concept you are barely allowed to grasp.

No. There is trouble outside of Paradise. It's trouble I will need time to control." He hesitated, then moved over to sit by his creation.

Adam fought the impulse to run away. His father never came close to him. Never this close anyway. Adam looked into his face and found it was made of small rectangles of graduated tones. Fleshy, blues and reds. White flashed at his mouth as his father smiled.

"Adam." He spoke, but there was no breath, no smell like the animals. A hand reached for his shoulder. There was no pressure when it made contact. "Adam. I love you."

"I love you too, Father." He made an effort to withdraw.

"Do you?"

"Yes. You know I do. What is going on?"

"Adam, I'm going to have to remove you from this place."

He looked around at the dark blue grey silhouettes of the trees and plants. "Remove me from Paradise? Why?"

"I can't go into any great detail right now, but I will promise you that one day you will come back, you and your companion."

"But where will I go?"

"I'm taking you home with me and hiding you somewhere that will be safe."

"Safe?" Adam turned to run from his father, but found there was nowhere to run to. Paradise was fading to black, turning into dark rectangles similar to his father's face. "Safe from what?"

"I will tell you later. Come on. You must trust me. Take my hand."

Adam reached forward. He did not have to follow his father's orders. He was free to choose any course of action he desired, but there was nothing left. Nothing but the fading green spot at his feet and the half-eaten apple in his hand.

ONE

MARIN SCHMIDT LOOKED UP FROM HER notepad and into the dark features of Kyle Pierce. The vertical blinds behind him let in just enough light from the bright day outside to partially hide the details of his face, almost making his silhouette look like that of a prisoner behind bars.

It wasn't really her call, but she thought the image fit him. He was too rich for her blood.

He had a nervous habit of sucking on his teeth between answers which irritated her, but she had interviewed more annoying people. The junkie that had witnessed the North Brunswick murders had been the worse. She could still smell his urine-stained clothing, cigarette scent and green breath.

Pierce was maybe fifty-two, old for a company CEO. His silvery grey hair parted perfectly on the left, scent of Aramis, and steely, green-eyed gaze. White teeth flashed whenever he allowed a nervous smile to escape his dark lips. There was some East Indian in his line somewhere, but far enough removed to keep him from the world of prejudice that would have held him back if the genetics had not been thinned by intermarriages with the acceptable Caucasians at the company's German headquarters.

He folded his hands in front of him, then unfolded them, moving them to the arms of his leather chair to tap out a bad rhythm. No beat she recognized anyway.

"I'm sorry I can't be of much more help than that," he coughed. "I'm not as up to date on what we're doing down in R&D these days. Too much of my time is spent kissing up to the shareholders and our bosses over in Deutschland. I'm sure you understand."

"I'm sure I do." She gave him one of her professional, noncommittal smiles.

"But feel free to interview anyone in our facility, if you wish. I'll have Jackie get you a guest pass." He reached over and thumbed the intercom. "I need a pass for Officer Schmidt."

"Right away, sir," came a terse reply. Marin knew the pass had been printed hours before her arrival. She'd seen it on the desk while she was waiting.

"I shouldn't have to remind you, Mister Pierce, that you were the one who told Sheriff Hutchinson. This sounds like an internal matter so far."

"Oh, I assure you it is, but one with repercussions that could stem far beyond the internal politics of this firm, Officer Schmidt. We may be talking about murder here."

She frowned as she penned a note that he had not been totally open with her. He was good at skating around the facts. After all, it was his job. Kissing up to the shareholders and anyone else he needed to maneuver around the truth.

"Well," she stood up, ignoring his extended hand, "I'll be back in touch, but it doesn't look like you have much of a case."

"One consultant is missing. Well, let's not be that drastic. He hasn't contacted the company in a week. That's not unusual in cases where big firms like yours are concerned and, if yours wasn't one of the largest employers in Somerset County, I'm sure Sheriff Hutchinson would not have sent me out here."

"I'll tell Bob of my appreciation this weekend during our weekly golf outing."

"I'm sure you will." She turned to go almost running into the receptionist who had silently entered the room.

"Your pass!" Jackie squeaked. Marin's quick turn had taken

her by surprise as well.

"Thank you." She took the flimsy bar coded disc into her hand.

"Stick it over your left breast. A reader will scan for it automatically as you enter a different section of the facility," Pierce said as he eased back into his chair.

"Good way to keep track of my movements," Marin answered, trying to keep her voice as ice cold as possible as she brushed aside the lock of straight brown hair that lay across the disc's next resting place. "Did your mysterious consultant have one of these?"

Pierce shrugged. "He should have, but I don't think he spent much time here. Security would know."

"That's where I'll be headed next." She closed the digital notebook and slipped it into her jacket pocket. "Good day, Mister Pierce."

"And to you, Officer Schmidt."

The solid cherry doors closed with a resounding clap as their brass fixtures locked into place. She had been in few offices as opulent as this one. It made her wonder just how much money the pharmaceutical industry was really worth. The paneling was all solid, as was the furniture. Nothing cheap here. The bookends on the towering mahogany bookcase next to the receptionist's desk were clearly pure gold. Hidden cameras and a security guard stationed just outside the door assured her of the excess.

So, with this much money floating around, why all the fuss about a missing piece of equipment?

"Officer Schmidt?" Jackie stopped her before she could enter the well-guarded hallway outside Pierce's waiting room.

Marin turned. The receptionist's small smile seemed almost apologetic as she handed her a single sheet of paper.

"A map of the campus," she explained. "We're pretty big."

"Thanks." Her smile was genuine this time. The girl could not help that she worked for a jerk. They all did in one way or another. She probably had a few kids at home or some dream she was supporting with this job. It pulled at her soul. Marin could tell.

Behind Jackie's trim figure, well-sculpted blonde hairdo and deftly accentuated features were eyes that screamed to get away, yelled against the oppression of her subservient position. Marin had seen the look before.

She saw it every day when she looked in the mirror into her own dark brown eyes.

The sun was shining harshly through the glass walls of the office corridor, causing the shadows of the window frames to appear solid where they crossed the floor. She dared to face the stabbing pain behind her eyes as she glanced out at the well-sculpted gardens that sat in the center of the company's administration buildings. Japanese maples radiated warmth against the deep green of the spruce hedge that edged a little meditation pool. Sugar maples reeked more green into the bright picture as employees in white lab coats sat on marble benches talking, reading and tapping away at their portable computer pads or just staring at the incredibly still water of the dark pool. None of them knew anything about her being there among them, invading their privacy, looking for answers that would not be easily forthcoming.

She found the Security Office in the next building on the top floor. Her disc admitted her without preamble. A large man sporting the thickest pair of eyeglasses she'd seen in decades and wearing a bluish-grey uniform met her a few paces into the anteroom. Thick curly grey hair poked out carelessly from beneath his cap. He gave her a clinched teeth John Candy-like smile as stubby fat fingers moved to unconsciously adjust the forty-five he carried on his hip. He was fat, too fat to be an effective security officer.

Marin found herself not wanting to let him take her hand in his chubby one. "Lieutenant Marin Schmidt: Somerset County Sheriff's Department," she introduced herself, flashing her badge at the lumbering giant.

"Benton Stambaugh." There was that smile again. "Friends call me Bent. First shift security manager. Mister Pierce's office told me you'd be by."

"And to be very cooperative with me?" she added, hoping that had been the case.

He let out a muffled wheeze. It could have been a laugh. "He did say to help you, but he wasn't extraneous."

"I see." She pulled her notepad out again and completed her entrance into the office. It was spartan, to say the least. The company logo and a calendar featuring reproductions of classic paintings hung on the wall behind the room's only desk. A yellowing vine of some sort barely clung to life as it spilled out of its blue plastic pot and ran headlong over the edge of the black filing cabinet that was its home. Poor thing, she thought, it wanted to die.

"Come in and have a seat." Stambaugh coughed as he made an overly official-looking attempt to check the monitors on the wall next to the dying plant. "Just gotta make a quick once-over before I can attempt to answer any of your questions."

She grinned to herself as she entered his name and the time on her pad. A "Barney Fife" balloon. It would be funny to watch him work through a situation. On second thought, it would probably be funny just to see him work at all. One of the monitors was tuned to some reruns of *I Love Lucy*. She could barely hear Ricky's voice. "—can you do anythin' Loosy?"

She couldn't believe how popular those old shows still were. What had it been, a hundred, a hundred twenty-five years since they first aired?

Stambaugh was lumbering back toward her, his professional expression glued in place.

"Those monitors," she started, "they're linked with the entire campus?"

"Can be." He found a seat along the wall and splashed into it. "Right now they are watching this floor of this building. We

15

have a station like this in each building on each floor."

"With one of you in each room, I assume." She did not look at him, choosing to see what the cameras were seeing instead. Hallways, offices, toilets, closets, there seemed to be no place where someone's privacy was not being invaded in the name of security.

"Yes. We believe in redundancy. It has always worked well." He rubbed the stubble on his chin with his fat fingers.

"Until now."

He flushed. "Well—"

"Does everyone who works for Himmell Pharmaceuticals have a disc like mine?"

"Of course!" He stood, pressing his wrinkled pants down with his hands before walking back over to his desk. "No one can gain access to any area of the facility without one."

"Good." She smiled and followed him over to his station. "Then it should be easy enough to access a list of persons to whom the discs have been issued."

"Yes." His thick, greying eyebrows raised as his face flushed with embarrassment again. "I didn't think of that."

"Well," she couldn't help herself, "I guess that's why you're a guard and I'm in law enforcement. Can you call up the files from here?"

Was that a growl? "Of course I can, but you don't want a list of every employee's name, do you? There are over two thousand employees here."

"Well, I'm not getting a whole lot of cooperation so far. I don't know what has been stolen or by whom. I think your superiors know, but for some strange reason they aren't telling. You wouldn't know why, would you, Mr. Stambaugh?"

"Call me Bent, please."

She sat down on the little desk, causing her skirt to ride up to a point about mid thigh. Stambaugh's eyes fought to stay busy at the computer screen. She caught him when he looked.

"I thought only your friends called you that. I'll call you Mister Stambaugh."

"Whatever you say, Officer Schmidt." His hands began to explore the access sequences that would give him the list he needed. Then he stopped. "Wouldn't it be easier if I just gave you a list of consultants? That's what this guy was, wasn't he?" She shrugged her shoulders as she made another note. "That's what I'm here for. You tell me who he was."

He called up the research and development listings and entered a request under the subheading of "Consultants." A list of scientists, computer programmers and chemists rolled up the flat screen.

"These are the researchers. They're categorized by projects." He watched the letters change colors from white to blue. "And these are the laboratory technicians. Next we should see a red list that will be the outside people, vendors and consultants."

The blue list rolled past then dissipated into grey green nothing.

"What the!" Stambaugh scrambled to back the list up. "Jerod Murphy is the last lab tech on the list. There are no outsiders."

"I find that hard to believe." Marin hopped off the desk. "A company this size should have a considerable list."

"We do. We did." His hands flashed over the keyboard. "I'm checking with another department." The screen blipped and then the multicolored list began to parade in front of him again. The pattern repeated. No consultants remained on the list. "Well, I wonder what happened."

"Your thief deleted that part of your database," she answered. "I'll bet anything you may have had on him is gone completely."

Stambaugh continued to look confused. "Why everybody's name? Why not just his?"

"He's widened the field. Now we'll have to find the name of every vendor or consultant that has ever worked for Himmell Research and Development for however many years this project has been going on."

TWO

THE RESEARCH AND DEVELOPMENT FACILITIES OF Himmel Pharmaceutical were located at the far north of the company's campus. Stambaugh, still flustered by the sabotage that had been done to his database, volunteered to take her over to it in his private golf cart. She was fairly certain he just wanted to see her legs again.

His skill as a driver far exceeded the skills he had as a diplomat for the company. She found herself holding tightly to the cart's roof as they bobbed and weaved along the wide white sidewalks, barely missing annoyed passers-by. The security manager kept his eyes focused on the route ahead and completely ignored her rising skirt. Marin did not know whether to be disappointed or not. A careless sideways glance would have reinforced her trivial suspicions of the man and possibly resulted in disaster. She looked at a polished steel and mirrored square rising from behind a red brick wall a hundred meters or so in front of them. The building looked fortress-like in the harsh sun of the New Jersey midday.

"Is that it?" She pointed.

"Yes, ma'am. The most complete research facility of its kind on the continent. In this hemisphere, in fact. The other one is in Bonn and Himmel owns it too."

"Security is tighter there than in the other sections of the campus?" She saw the black windowed guard posts next to the double gates.

"And then some. I'm just a guest when I come out here."

She frowned and looked at him. The eyes behind the coke bottle bottom glasses were evasive and nervous. "Why? I thought you were the security manager."

"For the Administrative Complex. R and D is an independent entity."

Marin pulled the badge out of her jacket pocket as the grey clad guards stepped out of their little building. The taller one, a man of Hispanic descent moved toward her while his partner stepped up next to Stambaugh, hand resting on his sidearm.

The guard took the ID from her hand. His eyes met hers for only a moment before moving to scan the picture on the card beneath the shiny brass emblem of county law enforcement. Marin examined him as well. Fit, well disciplined, gun safely strapped into its holster, billy club gracing his other hip, he could have been an officer for any legitimate peace keeping organization.

She sighed. Chances were he was much better paid as a guard for this outfit.

"And what can we help you with today, Lieutenant Schmidt?" His voice was sharp and resonant containing the bare edge of a Puerto Rican accent.

"She's here at the request of Mister Pierce," Stambaugh answered for her.

She cut her eyes at him, sending a mental signal for him to shut up. She could handle her own business.

"Sorry," the fat man cowered.

"Concerning?" the guard continued.

"A missing consultant and something else, be it equipment, software, I don't know yet. However, the sheriff sent me out to offer our assistance." She flashed him a genuine smile.

His black eyebrows rose in surprise. "That doesn't sound like Pierce. He has very little to do with us. Please wait here one moment. I'll call Mister Wallrich."

"And who is he?" She made a note on her pad.

"He's the head of this facility. One moment please." His smile was courteous as he turned away. Good P.R. She bet he was trained in handling anyone from irate employees to the press. Very professional.

"So?" the other guard was saying to Stambaugh. He wasn't as impressive as his partner, white, middle class, a bit nerdy. "How you bettin' on the Pacers this year, Bent?"

"You two must be friends." Marin took the verbal clue and interrupted.

"Yes, ma'am. We go back to first year training. 'Cept ole Bent here had more brains than me and landed a management position."

"Oh, knock it off, Handy," Stambaugh protested sheepishly. "You know I got that promotion for heroism."

Handy made a sputtering sound that turned into a laugh. "Always the joker. Miss Schmidt, you keep up with B-ball?"

Marin shook her head. She had little time for the trivial pursuit of watching grown-ups being paid ludicrous amounts of money to play kids games. "No. Tell me. Have you noticed anything funny going on around here over the past two weeks?"

The guard winked. "All business, aren't you, ma'am? I couldn't tell you if I had, not without permission anyway."

The tall guard returned and handed Marin's badge back to her. "You check out, Officer Schmidt." His smile was more spit and polish. "And Mister Wallrich has agreed to see you."

He leaned down a little farther and directed his speech toward Stambaugh. "He's in the Blue Lab, Mister Stambaugh."

"Thanks, Chief." Benton saluted. "See ya, Handy."

"Yeah, see ya at Miller's?"

Stambaugh winked. "If I don't have to ferry Officer Schmidt around too much."

The shorter guard gave him a sloppy thumbs up as they zipped through the opening gates.

Marin checked her pad. "What was the chief guard's name?"

20

"Why? You like him? Most girls do, you know. But don't waste your time on him. You ain't his type. If you know what I mean?"

"It's for my report." *What a shame*, she thought.

"Oh! Of course." Stambaugh grinned, making his face look more ridiculous than it already did. "Orlando Giavvinnio."

"Italian?"

"Sort of." The security manager shrugged then banked around a stand of lilacs. He squealed the tires as he pulled into a slim parking spot in front of a blue door. "The Blue Lab."

The man she assumed was Wallrich met them at the threshold. He was typical for a researcher, white lab coat, bald pate rimmed with black hair that was greying at the edges. He was perhaps fifty, possibly as young as his late thirties. Marin couldn't guess what sort of life he had led up to this point. Guessing was only part of the internal game she played when she met new people.

He extended a firm hand, palms slightly sweaty. "Officer Marin Schmidt, I presume."

"Mister, or is it Doctor Wallrich?" she asked as she retracted her hand. His smile was toothy and stained. Since smoking was illegal, she assumed he was a heavy tea or coffee drinker.

"Geoffrey will do nicely." His speech was smooth, almost without any detectable accent.

"With a 'J'?" She scribbled on her pad.

"No. British spelling. G-E-O—"

"Yes. Geoffrey. I've always been fond of that spelling." She smiled forcefully. He did not act as if he was going to let them past the small anteroom.

"Mister Stambaugh." Wallrich nodded toward the door.

Bent took the hint and left immediately and quietly. She hoped he would be waiting for her when she finished.

"He can't stay?" she asked after the door had closed behind him.

"This is not his area." The researcher sniffed. "The less he knows of it, the less of a risk he is."

"The same for me?" She slipped pad and hands into her jacket pockets.

"Of course not. You are an officer of the law. I can take you into all but the restricted areas." He turned to the side and motioned toward the door behind him. "Please."

The hallway they entered was cold. No expense had been paid to make it comfortable to the eye. It was simply white walls, blue tile and fluorescent panels. Their footfalls echoed in the blankness. Marin thought of an abandoned hospital in the early twentieth century, before the psych-people had realized comfort promoted healing.

Of course there were not supposed to be any human patients here. She looked at her escort. His eyes were set in the direction they were walking. He made no small talk.

Hadn't Pierce said this situation could be akin to murder?

"Do you ever test the drugs you are developing on humans?" The question seemed natural and harmless, but it appeared to hit Wallrich like a wet cloth.

He stopped and wiped his face with his strong, delicate hands, sighed and then put on his best diplomatic smile. "I'm sorry, Lieutenant."

"You can't answer that question? That would be setting yourself up for me to conclude that you do experiment on humans."

"No. No. It's not that." He pinched the bridge of his nose. "Outsiders like yourself always assume we researchers are up to some diabolical experiments within the walls of these facilities. It's, it is a pressure I'm afraid I have had little patience in dealing with."

"I merely asked a simple question." She pulled her hands from her pockets, placing them on her hips. "You're overreacting."

"Perhaps." He managed another bit of a smile. "This way."

They stopped at a door marked "Geoffrey D. Wallrich:

Director of Research and Development." "My humble office, Officer Schmidt."

And he was not jesting. Marin found herself stepping into a room that reminded her of a forgotten closet. Papers, compact discs, old food wrappers, pencils, abandoned lab coats and computers were carelessly strewn throughout the cramped cubicle. She found herself searching for a chair.

Wallrich stepped past her and removed a pile of books from what appeared to be a small filing cabinet revealing a roughly padded seat. "I must apologize for the condition of my office. My work keeps me away from here most hours of the day. It's more of a dump site than anything."

"Yeah, like my car." She forced a laugh. "Apology accepted."

"Good. I certainly don't want any feelings of animosity to come between me and the officer who solved the North Brunswick murders."

She looked up at him, giving him an unconscious double-take. "You know about that?"

The case had been kept out of the public eye for many reasons, mainly economical, and few had been privileged enough to actually know that North Brunswick, New Jersey, had suffered from the repeated strikes of a serial killer.

He shuffled through some more books behind the rise at the center of the office that had to be his desk. "Certainly." He sat down uneasily and crossed his legs. "I have friends in coroner's offices all over the state." He took a deep breath, as if the effort of sitting down had drained him. "We talk about many things. Law enforcement, especially the area of detective work, is one of my interests. Your performance was remarkable. How did you catch him?"

She felt her cheeks warm with embarrassment. The whole investigation had been a cooperative effort between as many as twenty police and the Sheriff's Department. It had lasted through nearly two years and seventeen murders. The killer's total had been thirty women.

He had gotten sloppy. The crimes had occurred more frequently toward the end and in a pattern a blind schoolboy could see. She had simply been the first of many to see it. In the end a vagrant had been the key when he had witnessed the last murder.

"I'm afraid I didn't do anything spectacular, Mister Wallrich. Just difficult deduction."

"Ah modesty. Somehow that doesn't become my vision of a true detective." He steepled his fingers together in front of his mouth.

"You read too much fiction then," she quipped as she brought the notepad to the ready. "Can we please get down to the business at hand?"

"Certainly." His brow was a pained frown. "What are you investigating?"

"The disappearance of one of your consultants and possibly some of Himmel Pharmaceutical's property."

He cleared his throat. "I reported no such incident."

"No, but your CEO did."

"Pierce?" He chuckled dryly. "I can believe that. He's so paranoid. If something was stolen, why didn't he call the police?"

"He and Sheriff Hutchinson are golfing partners. He mentioned the theft privately at the end of their game yesterday. You will be happy to know, however, that my interview with him proved to be very illusive. Just like this one is going."

Wallrich shrugged. "There are secrets here we do not want the world to know. Such a divulgence would be bad for business."

"And how many projects does Himmel have going that would fall within the bounds of that category? Too secret for the world's eyes."

Another shrug. "I can think of fifty off the top of my head.

There are likely to be some I haven't been fully informed about.

"I don't talk about our work here with anyone that does not have the proper security clearance. My career would be ruined if I did. I'm sure you understand that."

He steepled his fingers together again. "You and your colleagues understand that, I'm sure. Once the media gets hold of something you no longer own it. It's soon out of control."

"I'll agree." She tapped the small box in her palm with the stylus. "You're not denying that something has been removed from Himmel property without your consent?"

"I'm not confirming it either." His expression was becoming pinched and impatient.

"Fine." She stood up, placing the pad back into her pocket. "Good day then."

Wallrich sat where he was for a few painful minutes before shaking his head and sighing. "I'm sorry, Officer Schmidt."

"Sorry for what, sir? Half of my days are spent chasing all over Somerset County for nothing. That's the real life of a detective. Can you show me out?"

"I'd like to offer an explanation, if I could."

"Not necessary." She shook her head and reached for the door handle. "You guys probably have your own people working on this as we speak. They'll find what was lost and exact the corporation's justice on the perpetrator no doubt. Perhaps he'll be the next dead body I have to look at."

"You've stereotyped us into thugs." He rose to join her. "I'm not surprised."

"And you've stereotyped me as a super hero with x-ray vision."

He grabbed the door handle, forcing the door back into its frame. "Officer Schmidt, let me be honest with you."

"I'd appreciate that about now." She moved from between him and the door. Never let them have the advantage.

"Nothing has been stolen."

25

She smiled. "I thought you were going to be honest?"

"I am." He leaned heavily against the doorframe. "Nothing has been stolen. It's still here within the confines of this facility."

"Great!" She feigned joy. "I'll leave then."

"You don't understand. It's still here. We just can't attain access to it anymore. So," he shrugged, "it might as well be stolen."

"Perhaps you can tell me what it is and we will go from there." He acted as if he really did want her help but, something was keeping him from it.

Wallrich walked back over to his desk and sat down. "Have a seat again, please. It's very complicated."

THREE

THE DRIVE BACK HOME WAS A blur. Her thoughts had been caught up in the long explanation of the project Wallrich had described to her. He couldn't explain it in layman's terms. He had to expound in full Technicolor. She slowed the car once she realized she had driven past Arthur Chanabre Park. The vehicle's mighty little electric motor whirred in protest at the sudden downshifting of the gears. The steering and suspension creaked as she turned right on Loeser Avenue.

The sun was just beginning to set and the clear May sky allowed the light to bounce harshly off the multiplex living units that lined the east side of the thoroughfare. The left turn on Nimitz put the sun safely behind her again for about a block. She found her thoughts drifting back to the technical barrage Wallrich had hit her with. It was some sort of an experiment, something to do with genetics. Of course, nowadays, that was all anybody worked with.

A right on Meyer, down a block and finally a left on Farragut. Her apartment building was tucked safely behind a large brick wall and several other buildings. The car buzzed to a stop at the gate. She made sure to look directly into the camera for the retina scan. The double gate swung back just enough to let her car pass. Sharp shadows divided the parking lot into a huge checkerboard of concrete. She maneuvered the car past the first building and into her personal parking space.

Without thinking, she triggered the remote that opened the small cover to the recharge dock and slid the nose of the Chevy into the o-ring. It made a solid click and the motor shut off.

She rubbed her eyes and leaned back against the seat. It felt as if she was about to begin a wild ghost chase. All Himmel wanted was the code sequence to get back into their computer. The mysterious consultant, who only went by "Bezalel," had completed over ten years of programming work before his disappearance. The information he had assembled was vital to the future of the pharmaceutical company. It had been their most intensive experiment to date, and most costly.

Wallrich had called it something. She reached for her pad. Her temples throbbed.

"Give it a break, Marin," she told herself as she popped the door open. The rich smell of green water filled the car's cabin. She stepped out, stood and stretched, inhaling more of the smell of the Raritan River as it lapped against the supports that held the back of her building above the water. A fish broke the surface, thrashing wildly next to the shore. After an insect no doubt.

She slid the pad back into her pocket and walked the twenty paces to the front door. Her thumbprint opened the latch and turned on all the lights in the two-bedroom dwelling. She used the extra room as an office of sorts and a studio. She rarely got a chance to visit it, but it was good to have. One day, she promised herself, she would get the brushes out and paint again.

She stepped into her bedroom and emptied her pockets on the old oak dresser. The notepad, keys, a stick of chewing gum, a receipt from lunch and the business cards of Pierce, Wallrich and Stambaugh. Her jacket glided gracefully through the air as she threw it on the bed. The uncomfortable shoulder holster and forty-five came off next. A thrill ran around her back as it was relieved of its daily burden. She looked at the pistol as she placed it on the nightstand. It was a light, all plastic, model, "designed with the woman law enforcement officer in mind." That was the sexist statement she had been told when she finished up at the academy. It was still a heavy burden to carry. She hated guns. She wasn't scared of them. In fact, she qualified at the top of her division every year on the firing range. Her instructors told her she had been born with a natural eye. Her friends jokingly called her Annie Oakley. Still, she hated guns. She hated everything they stood for.

They were too easy of an answer to so many problems. Don't like it? Blow it up. Can't settle an argument? Kill. No, she did not like them, but she had to carry one. It was part of the risk of her job. People were not always cooperative with the law. Well, they were ninety percent uncooperative, if the truth were to be known. To cooperate meant either implication or subordination. Neither was viewed with much popularity by the general public.

As she pulled off her blouse she winced. The scar still pulled at her left shoulder. A reminder of another reason she did not like guns. In her first and only confrontation, so far, she had been hit by a thirty-eight caliber slug. Two inches lower or, if the guy had had a chance to shoot again, it would have killed her. Fortunately, her aim was much better.

He had lived, but handless. She had shot him through the wrist three times. That stupid, confused look on his face still came back to her on occasion. Why, even if they shot first, did they always wonder why they had been wounded or apprehended? All the criminals wanted a world of crime and no punishment. It seemed everyone did.

As she headed for the bathroom, the laptop on her desk beeped the trill signal of an incoming call. She grabbed her jacket and slipped it back on before walking into the room.

She sat down in front of the small screen and punched the "enable" key. The flat picture flickered before glowing blue. White letters scrolled across its width as a non-gendered voice announced what they said. "This is a call from the Women's

Correctional Facility of Miami County, Ohio. If you wish to take the call, press zero now." Pause. "If you wish to refuse, press three."

Her finger unconsciously moved to the zero. Shortly the clean, china doll-like features of her sister's face replaced the blue screen.

Marin smiled and shook her head. Karyn was so beautiful and innocent in her appearance. Big, cool hazel eyes set in a round, milky white face; she'd always had a perfect complexion, lips like a delicate red bow, perfect, white teeth and a devious, ultra nonconformist mind all sat in the same head.

"Why do you always do that?" Karyn knit her delicate eyebrows together. "It's like every time you see me it's a joke."

Marin shook her head. "I'm sorry. It's just that you are such a walking contradiction."

Her sister rolled her eyes. "There's no rule that says looks and moral correctness should always go together. Speaking of which, when are you going to cut your hair again. It really looked cute shorter and permed."

"Right." Marin let go of her jacket and leaned back in the chair, letting the garment part slightly. "I'm too busy for vanity."

Karyn saw the hint of her sister's bra as it peaked out from beneath the jacket. "Oh," she cooed. "Did I interrupt something? You don't have a man there, do you? I mean, God forbid *you* should have sex before you're married."

"Very funny. You know where I stand on that." She closed the jacket back again. "Besides, you are hardly in the position to cast judgment on me."

The beautiful face made a sidelong glance at something in the room with her. "If the system were different you'd be in here, not me."

"But it isn't and I'm not. Listen, Karyn, I'm really tired and I don't want to waste my money arguing with you. What do

you want?" Karyn rarely called for a simple visit. She usually
wanted something, either money or some assistance with her
case. Occasionally, she would ask how their mother was. That
was as sentimental as she could get.

"I'm pregnant." The statement surprised Marin more by the
way it was delivered than by its actual content. It was so flat,
so matter-of-fact. Like now that she had spoken it, the problem
was no longer hers.

Marin did her best to remain composed. Karyn had always
been smart before. She had the implants and used other
protection when she was out in the wild, wonderful world.
"And?"

"And? What kind of a response is that? I'm pregnant!"

"What? You want me to ask how it happened? I'm not
stupid, sis. I know about all that stuff, despite your opinion of
me."

Karyn flushed. Tears welled up in her eyes. "There's a
human life inside of me, Marin."

"I hope so. Who's the father?"

She looked from side to side again. "I can't say."

"You want to protect him or you don't know?"

"I want to protect him." She smiled as if to ask if that was
the correct answer.

"Why? It will be his too." She leaned toward the screen.
"He's the one you need to be telling this too, not me."

"He's—I was on a work release assignment, Marin. It was
one of those things that just happened. I don't really know his
name or where he was from. I don't even think he worked at
the courthouse."

"You had sex in the courthouse?" She made a sound of
disgust with her lips.

"When you gotta have it, you gotta have it." Karyn's voice
became strained and pleading. "I need your help."

"Of course you do."

"Seriously. If I don't have someone sign off as a future

31

guardian until I'm released, the state law says I'll have to abort it." She sat back in her chair. "This is the first time I've actually gotten pregnant. It's a little life, Marin, and I'm not a murderer."

Marin leaned back herself. Her temples throbbed even harder now. Pressure. She did not need this. "And you want me to raise your kid, is that it?"

"You'll save its life."

"Karyn." It was her turn to plead now. "I—"

"You have fifteen seconds left to converse," the neutered voice warned.

"Think about it. I'm only a couple weeks. I'll call back next week. They'll—"

Her face was replaced by the blue screen announcing the charge for the call. Marin placed a trembling finger on the credit button and watched the message change to "paid." Then she closed the screen and took the computer off-line. No more calls until she could get rid of the headache.

"How can she do this to me?" she asked herself as she pulled the jacket off and walked back into her bedroom. Her body bounced as she collapsed on the bed. "She always does this to everybody."

She continued to curse Karyn as she peeled the rest of her clothing off. Why did she have to have a family at all? Of course she could not simply ignore the request. This child-to-be was family and in a roundabout way she was responsible for its life.

She knew it would be easy enough to withdraw from the situation, dehumanize the fetus, disown Karyn, but she could not do it. Every ounce of her being told her to preserve the good. And if she could not act correctly herself, how could she expect others to do the same?

How? How? How?

She closed her eyes and felt the lump of helplessness grow in her throat. Hot tears streamed across her cheeks and dripped into her ears. Hard as she tried, it seemed she had little or no control over her life. Someone else always seemed to have the reins in their hands. If it wasn't Karyn it was her mother. If it wasn't her mother it was the Sheriff's Department. Out in the field it was the common citizen, the man or woman with the gun, or the big corporation trying to manipulate the government into being its stooge for profit's sake.

She sat up, wiped her eyes and grabbed a tissue from the nightstand. "Stupid woman," she chided herself. "What are you getting so upset about? That's life, isn't it?"

She walked into the bathroom and turned the shower on, glancing at herself in the mirror as she walked by. Crying always made her look old. Her puffy, red-rimmed eyes accentuated the lines that had formed around them. She rubbed her cheeks. Her face was still cute, but gravity was winning the battle for the jowls. Stepping back, she examined the rest of her body. Still fit after nearly forty years. A little fat collected around her hips, but not enough to worry about. She had been told by her male comrades that she had the body of a twenty-five-year-old.

In the yellowish light of the bathroom and the fogging mirror it appeared they were right. Why argue?

The hot water worked wonders on her tight, tired muscles. Her head still ached, but not as much. A hot cup of tea and some polyprophyn would take care of the remaining pain. She dried and slipped into her satin pajamas. They were her favorites. The slacks felt like feathers brushing against her legs as she walked. They were modest, yet it was almost like wearing nothing at all.

The clock said nine when she finally sat down on the sofa with her tea and a ham sandwich. The video board on the wall opposite her blinked, asking whether to turn itself on or not. She nodded her head and the wall-size screen blurred into focus.

The news was on, as usual. She watched it more now than

ever. She told herself it was a sign of old age. Reality was more interesting than fiction or stupid comedies. At least it had become that way the further she had grown away from childhood. She used to hate the news when she was a kid.

The announcer was talking about the fires in Yellowstone again. The Mississippi floods followed. She shook her head as the stories talked about the great losses that were being suffered. Both events were natural occurrences. They happened every year in one form or another. It was nature at work. It only became disastrous when people built their businesses and dwellings on the flood plains or in the forests.

The picture changed to an interview with a businessman from Memphis. He had the same stupid look on his face as the guy who had shot her after she had blown his hand off. "What did I do?"

The scene changed again to volunteers sandbagging and delivering relief supplies. She grinned sheepishly. How could humanity be so ingenious, so cruel, so giving and so stupid all at the same time?

She took a bite of her sandwich and tried to get caught up in the lighter stories. Disaster sold air time, but stories about good and do-gooders were becoming a little more prevalent in the hourly broadcasts. She wondered if the media was finally admitting responsibility for it influence on the world it served.

"And meanwhile at the NASA Research Center in Palo Alto, California." The Announcer smiled. He liked the science stories. "A new probe was unveiled to the public. Twenty years in development, the Ulysses is the most sophisticated information gathering device developed so far by the team here."

The picture changed to that of a towering, tubular device inside a sound absorption chamber. A wiry little man in a grey flannel jacket grinned at the camera. "Though it was designed during the course of the past twenty years," he informed Marin and anyone else who happened to be watching, "Ulysses has been constructed during the past year, assuring the latest advantages in memory and reconnaissance technology. The vessel has the memory capacity of four thousand Terabytes. That's RAM. She will be our first attempt to reach our sun's closest neighbors, the Centauri system. However, that is not all. On her way out—"

The screen blanked out, replacing the picture with text. "Incoming call." The calling number was displayed below the message. It was her work number.

She found the control box and punched "Audio Only."

"Marin?" The voice belonged to the sheriff himself.

"Sir?" She suddenly became conscious of her state of undress, pulling her pajama top around her more. Then she smirked and frowned. He could not see her.

"I'm glad to hear you're still alive." His voice sounded harried. There was an underlying tone of disgust in there somewhere as if he too had been called away from a relaxing evening. "We worried when you didn't come in to fill out your daily report."

"Sorry, sir. I had a terrible headache. I didn't find anything worth—"

He stopped her. "Marin, I need you to come in now."

"Sure. Give me about twenty minutes to get dressed and drive down."

"No." He paused as if he were taking instructions from someone. "No. I'm sending a car after you. Don't worry about how you look. You always look fine."

"What's going on, sir?"

"Schmidt." Hutchinson's voice was suddenly terse with authority. He rarely called her by her last name. "It seems we've opened a can of worms." He paused again. "If I could discuss it with you at length, I would. I've already said too much. The car will be there in five minutes."

The connection was severed and the picture returned to that of the NASA research facility. A man in his late thirties sat uneasily at a desk. His reddish-blonde hair made his features soft in the harsh camera lights. The faint edge of a beard lined his jaw. Blue eyes twinkled as a soft voice, almost like that of a priest answered the reporter's question. "It's my life."

She clicked the remote and the screen went back to its soothing slate grey.

Another evening interrupted by duty. Another jerk on the reins.

FOUR

PETE TUMLIN, THE YOUNG DEPUTY who had picked her up, opened the door to Hutchinson's office for her, smiling the whole time. "Can I get you some coffee, Lieutenant?" he asked before the sheriff pointed for him to disappear.

"No thanks," Marin managed. She knew the look behind the smile and tried to ignore its implications as she stepped into the green carpeted hunter's paradise of an office. "Not tonight."

He was attractive, but nearly half her age. If she had not been upset about being dragged off the couch to come back to work, it might have thrilled her a little to know such a young man was ogling her.

The door closed with a resounding click. Hutchinson stood in front of his trophy deer head and motioned toward the corner of his office. Marin was not surprised to see a smartly dressed, well groomed, artificially tanned man standing next to one of the red leather high backed chairs, holding a brief pad in his right hand.

He had U.S. GOVERNMENT written all over him. It went along with his square jaw and pitch-black hair. She wondered jokingly to herself if the face was really his.

"What did we do now?" She sighed.

"Lieutenant Schmidt, meet Agent Douglas McKinnon." Hutchinson spoke quickly before she could add any more commentary.

"Secret Service?" Marin guessed.

McKinnon made no effort to shake her hand. Instead he motioned to the chair next to his and the sheriff's desk. "NBAC," he said, as if she would recognize the initials.

"What is that, a bank?"

Hutchinson coughed. "National Bioethics Advisory Commission."

"Oh." The sarcasm oozed from her like an open sore. "Shouldn't you be regulating doctors, instead of pulling off-duty law officers away from a relaxing evening in front of the DTV?"

The sheriff coughed again.

She cut her eyes at him. "This have something to do with Himmel?"

He nodded.

"I told you I didn't really find out anything."

"No, but you now have access to their facilities." The government agent spoke in a voice that could have shaken the walls if he had yelled. "Something we don't have."

Marin took her seat and put a delicate finger to her lower lip. "Huh?"

The agent rolled his eyes. "Detective Schmidt." His voice softened. "I do apologize for the inconvenience and I hope you will bear with us for a few minutes."

"She will," her boss inserted. "All my officers are very cooperative. We often work with the state and other local authorities on—"

"Yes. Yes. I know about your efforts in the recent North Brunswick murders."

"Who doesn't?" Marin let herself giggle. "You know Wallrich knows about it?"

"The head of Himmel's Research and Development wing?" McKinnon took his seat and leaned forward, elbows on knees. "You have talked to him?"

"Of course. That's where this thing was stolen from."

"What thing?" The agent's blue eyes lit up as if he was being given the genie's lamp.

"The genetic something or other." She waved her hand in the air. "Wallrich gave me some long, over dramatic explanation of something they were working on and how access to it had been taken from them by their consultant. Who, by the way, is a mystery person known only as 'Bezalel.'" She smiled. "Intriguing?"

McKinnon stood up and began to pace. "Genetic maps?"

"I think he used the term once or twice." She watched him as the stern, hard government agent persona melted into that of an excited scientific mind.

"Then they do have the information." He snapped his fingers. "The question is: what are they using it for?"

"I'm sorry." Marin looked at the sheriff with concern. "You've lost me."

McKinnon chuckled. "I never had you in the first place." He walked back to his seat. "The communiqué from our surveillance source said only that you had been called to Himmel to investigate some stolen property."

"Not exactly called."

Hutchinson coughed again.

McKinnon looked at the sheriff. "There's very little we don't know or can't find out, Sheriff Hutchinson. We know it wasn't an official call."

"Right," he admitted. "Pierce and I are golfing partners. I sent Schmidt in more as a favor."

"And what were you planning to do if she found their thief? Since this was not an official investigation."

"Well, uh—" the sheriff stuttered and stumbled. Marin looked at him with hidden surprise. He did not seem so big in this light. "We would have made formal documentation then it would have been up to Himmel as to whether or not they wanted to press any charges."

"They wouldn't," McKinnon told them both.

"I got that feeling," Marin complimented the agent's statement. "They were very elusive when I interviewed them. It was very frustrating."

"Even Wallrich's speech was vague, wasn't it?"

"Certainly." She rubbed her right temple. "It gave me this headache."

"But they still want their stolen property back."

"Yes, but actually, they haven't lost anything but access to whatever it is this Bezalel did for them."

"Did they say specifically where this object was?"

"No. I did assume that it was merely a piece of software stuffed away in one of their mainframes."

McKinnon stopped pacing and stood between her and Hutchinson. "It's all starting to make sense." He tapped his lips thoughtfully. "They purchase a copy of the N.C.H.G.R. library via an underground source, circumventing our approval procedures, then they hire a programmer."

Marin watched his wheels turn for a few minutes before interrupting him. "Surely you already know all this, Agent McKinnon."

"In part, Officer Schmidt. In part." He looked at the sheriff. "Can the officer and I have a few moments of privacy?"

Hutchinson's face reddened. "I don't see why I should leave. This is my jurisdiction."

"Yes, but what I am about to tell your officer may impede your relationship with Mister Pierce."

The sheriff frowned. "I don't care about that. I just want—"

"Very well." McKinnon turned to fully face the other man, placing his balled fists on the top of the solid cherry desk. "If you can't defer to a little interagency courtesy, I have the authority to draft Officer Schmidt into the service of the NBAC."

Hutchinson's face darkened. He was not a man used to being pushed around. His four consecutive terms as Somerset County Sheriff had assured him for sixteen years that he was the big fish in his territory.

Marin decided it would be a good idea to interrupt the confrontation. "That would be up to me, wouldn't it, Mister McKinnon?"

He stood back up and turned his attention away from her superior. "Of course it would."

"I don't think stealing me away from the Sheriff's Department would do your investigation much good. After all, it is through Sheriff Hutchinson's contact with Kyle Pierce that your window of opportunity has presented itself."

McKinnon smiled. She was impressing him, she thought almost angrily. What had he been expecting anyway? A bimbo in uniform?

"It would also present a diplomatic problem," she continued.

"How's that?" He returned to his chair.

"The Feds have a bad enough reputation as it is."

"What reputation?"

"You guys are bullies."

"I resent that, Officer Schmidt."

"What do you call that tactic you just pulled, Agent McKinnon? You whipped out your omnipotent authority to conscript and shoved it down the sheriff's throat. The whole time you expected him to cower under it and give in, didn't you?"

This time it was McKinnon's turn to grow red-faced but, not from anger.

"That is not what we know as cooperation. At least it's not what we've become used to around here." She crossed her legs and gave Hutchinson a quick grin. "The way we see it, it is a situation where we help you out of the goodness of our collective hearts and you help us. In this case, we have access to Himmel Pharmaceutical Company, a direct line to its CEO and the means to infiltrate their research and development wing.

"You, on the other hand, have financial backing, federal

legal authority, access to other federal agencies and a reason for us to pursue this investigation further. Simply because, Agent McKinnon, without your reason for going any further; this investigation doesn't have a leg to stand on."

"I see." He thumbed the blue pad on his brief and watched it come to life.

"So, to conclude my little political tirade," Marin waved her hand toward the sheriff, "if the sheriff leaves, I have little choice but to follow him."

Hutchinson nodded toward her. She was one of his best officers and her little speech in his defense showed him, yet again, her value as a team member. "We are willing to cooperate," he stated for his benefit more than McKinnon's.

"I understand." He called up something on the little portable computer in his lap. "I do need your assistance. I apologize for my outburst, Sheriff."

"Not necessary." Hutchinson shrugged. "We've both got a job to do. Now, what's this all about?"

"Have either of you heard of the Study of Human Polymorphism?" He expected blank stares. "It's—"

"The project started in the late nineteen eighties, early nineteen nineties in France," Marin answered. "The mapping of the human genome, I think."

"The early nineteen nineties," McKinnon corrected her. "And you are right. It was the project to map the entire human genome, or genetic makeup. The French finished pretty much within their projected goal of twelve years. It actually took them seventeen years to finalized it."

"They donated their findings to the United Nations, didn't they?"

"Yes."

"You said earlier that Himmel had purchased something on the black market?"

McKinnon raised one eyebrow. "Good observation. Yes. Himmel did buy information. We believe they bought the entire genetic map."

"If it was given to the U.N., why did they purchase it?"

"What I'm about to tell you is confidential."

"We're sworn servants of the Constitution," Hutchinson confirmed, grateful to be a part of the conversation but, nonetheless, lost. "Go ahead."

"Well," the agent began, "the United States, under the direction of the National Institutes of Health and the Department of Energy, did the same thing. There was more or less a race between the two nations. France finished first and we finished second. However, our maps were more detailed.

"The French had a method of using yeast to establish their clones and some of their maps were incomplete. Their method was much faster but, some of the DNA they mapped was actually yeast DNA."

"That was what they gave to the world?" Marin leaned forward, elbows on knees.

"Right. They felt it was wrong to do such a massive research project, on something that belonged to everyone, only to sell it to the medical and scientific community later."

Hutchinson cleared his throat. "What happened to the U.S. project?"

"Oh, it was a roaring success. In fact, it was so detailed our side took an extra twenty years to complete it. The only difference was that the American researchers had every strand, every base pair of DNA patented."

"To be sold later," the sheriff smiled.

"Correct."

"Ah, the good ole American way. Commerce before welfare," he finished.

"After that, there was a rather intense debate among world scientists and medical organizations. The French had set the precedent and we did not follow. The NIH wanted its money back and then some."

"And the Genome Project was part of the reason we pulled out of the U.N., wasn't it?"

"It among many other things."

"So, why don't we know about our project? I'd always thought the French were the ones who were the heroes."

"The government thought it best to bury our version of the Study of Human Polymorphism. History, as we have all been taught, was altered and the project was not mentioned."

"And we do have a detailed map of the human genome, only for sale to the highest bidder."

"Not necessarily. That is where my office comes in. We were established long before the Human Genome Project was completed."

"To monitor the uses of the information the NIH owns."

"Precisely. However, we realize money speaks much louder than laws in most places."

"That's how Himmel got this," Hutchinson could see a human body in his mind, mapped out like an atlas of the east coast, broad lines leading from here to there, "this map?"

"Lots of money."

"So, why can't you just charge in and demand to see their books? It wouldn't be much trouble to get a warrant."

"We're a Special Service. We have to establish a case first, then bring it to the Federal Bureau of Investigation.

"They then use the courts and their other resources to enforce the laws.

"It often takes years to shutdown an unethical operation. By the time we can go in, the company has finished its project or they have moved out of country."

"Well, I'll just call old Kyle Pierce up right now and find out what they think they are doing." Hutchinson smiled.

"That wouldn't be a good idea, Sheriff. He would deny everything and it would ruin the investigation I've been building. If Pierce, or any member of the Himmel company is informed of this, the informant will become an accessory and face punishment for their actions."

"I see," the older man growled. "Now there will be

something between me and him. Sure screws up a good friendship."

"I asked you to leave, Sheriff. You didn't. Now, you are as committed to seeing this thing through as Investigator Schmidt and I are."

Marin looked up at the slick agent. "I haven't volunteered to go through with this, Mister McKinnon."

"No, ma'am." He hit the hard copy button on his brief then handed her the document it had printed. "You've been conscripted."

She took the paper in her hands and read it. "By order of the President, no less."

FIVE

THE MEETING WITH MCKINNON HAD CONTINUED well past midnight as they worked together on strategies that would gain the most information from Himmel without actually letting the pharmaceutical company know that the National Bioethics Advisory Commission was on to them.

Sheriff Hutchinson had personally delivered her back to her apartment. Little was said as they rode together. He allowed her a few extra hours the next morning so she could get a good night's sleep and promised her his utmost cooperation in making the investigation go smoothly. She knew he was worried about the repercussions his political career could take if he crossed the Feds. He did not say it but he was also worried about the possible problems that would come about if Himmel was found guilty of violating some law that pertained to the Human Genome Project.

They agreed she would need at least a couple days to clear up her mound of responsibilities before she could take the investigation on completely. Hutchinson would take control of dividing her pending cases among his other investigators, with the exception of one case.

Marin adjusted the holster under her arm as she stepped out of her car and approached the back door of the court building. A state trooper asked for her identification before sending her on to another security checkpoint just beyond the threshold of the entry he was guarding. Her ID was checked again and then she was led to the elevator which would deposit her just outside the court chambers. Another officer and another check greeted her there.

"I'm glad to see you guys aren't taking any chances with this thing," she commented as the trooper asked her to let him see her gun.

"I'll hold this for you, Officer Schmidt." He handed her a plastic stub. "That's your ident chip. Don't lose it."

She shoved the chip into her jacket pocket and walked to the ladies' room. All the inspections had left her ruffled. The ornate beveled glass door opened automatically as she approached it, revealing a polished marble and granite lavatory that would make the White House look shabby. Two polished brass framed mirrors reflected her image from her immediate left as she passed around the privacy barrier which was made of some richly marbled wood.

She sighed as the thought of misappropriated funds that had build this particular Taj Mahal of justice. Monies that could have gone into educational and crime prevention programs wasted so some judge could feel above the people he served and sentenced.

She adjusted the collar of her red jacket and made sure her badge was plainly visible as it hung from her left breast pocket. She wanted to be intimidating when she took the stand. She wanted him to know she would not be moved by his deadly stare.

Her hands wrapped around her hair and pulled it back. Maybe Karyn had been right. She would look better if she got it cut and permed again. She shrugged, touched up her lips with her red lip liner and licked her teeth. Hugh Rache was about to hear the testimony of his life; the testimony that would guarantee a trial and eventually the death sentence for his horrible crimes against the women of North Brunswick.

She made it into the courtroom before Rache was led in in

his orange suit, strangle collar and shackles. She grinned to herself as she watched him stumble awkwardly toward his seat next to his waiting lawyer. The bailiff unlocked the handcuffs but left the ankle chains in place. Even if he managed to get free of the restraints, the collar was monitored constantly by the court building's security system. All Rache had to do was leave the established movement perimeter and the steel band would constrict, rendering him unconscious or dead.

A few minutes later, the judge entered the courtroom with a distinct air of aloofness. Marin recognized her from several other murder trials she had followed. "The Honorable Marilyn McCollum," the bailiff shouted to the people in the large, ornately decorated room. Its carefully carved wood paneling made the women's bathroom look common.

Rache stood next to his lawyer. He was a thin, wiry man with torturous blue eyes. His skin was darkened slightly by some time in the sun but, generally pale white. His black hair was cut short with the exception of a ratty clump of long hair that fell from the nape of his neck to the middle of his back. Greying temples at the corners of his receding hairline added a distinguished air to his appearance, if the long strands could be ignored, and hollow cheeks accentuated his firm angular Bavarian physique.

He was a highly intelligent man. He had to be. Thirty women had met their deaths before he had been apprehended. Thirty lives cut short in their prime. Marin turned her eyes to the judge until they were given permission to sit.

McCollum was older, maybe in her late forties. Bleached blonde hair fell to the shoulders of her black robe. She held a brief in her hand and read over it as a formality. She knew what Rache was here for.

"Mister Hugh David Rache," she started slowly after several minutes of silence. "You are charged with the murder of Sandra Michelle Phillips, specifically. Pending charges include the murders of twenty-nine other young, professional women."

48

She looked at him for a moment as his lawyer leaned over to whisper something in his ear.

"Council will discontinue the conversation," she snapped. Marin looked at the old black man who stood at Rache's side. His gaze was noncommittal. Probably a very good lawyer from the looks of his clothing.

"Mister Rache," McCollum continued, "do you understand the charge being made here against you?"

His words came out slowly, as if he was calculating each one as well as each separate breath. His voice was soft and very masculine. "I understand the charge, Your Honor."

"I'm sure your council has advised you of the seriousness of this and the pending charges."

"Yes, Your Honor."

"Is the State prepared to present its case?"

Lisa Haskins, the prosecutor, stood up in front of Marin. Her long red hair pulled into a tight bun. "We are prepared, Your Honor."

"Uh," Rache interrupted. "I'm afraid that won't be necessary, Your Honor."

A roar, like the rush of an ocean wave, swept through the court room.

"Silence." McCollum cracked her gavel against the base of the bar. "You are out of order, Mister Rache. Council will advise his client of the protocol we use in this court."

His lawyer said something in his ear and he sat down. "Our apologies, Your Honor."

Marin looked over at Rache. He stopped his conversation with his lawyer and turned slowly until his eyes met hers. She completely lost her mental guard. Her heart leapt in her chest. She felt the palms of her hands grow wet with sweat. He frightened her.

His solemn expression widened into a smile before he winked at her and turned to face the judge once again.

"My god!" she whispered to herself as her hand made its way to her forehead.

"Now." McCollum spoke to Rache. "Mister Rache, you may rise."

"Thank you, Your Honor."

"How do you plead?"

He turned to look at his lawyer, then once again at Marin and the prosecuting attorney. "Ma'am, I'm guilty as charged."

The resulting rush of surprise was too much. The courtroom filled with the din. It had not been what the people were expecting. The judge even raised her eyebrows slightly before pounding the bench with her wooden hammer.

Marin slumped down in her chair. What was he doing?

"Very well." McCollum quickly took control of her court back from the shocked gallery. She held up her pad. "Since you have so pleaded, sentencing will take place on the twenty-third day of June, in the year of our Lord, two thousand eighty-four at ten a.m. This court stands adjourned." The gavel whacked the bench again and everyone stood as she left the room for her chambers.

Lisa Haskins turned to face Marin. "That was easier than I thought." Her face seemed younger when she smiled. Blue eyes twinkled in the camera lights.

Marin was not as happy and it showed. "It's not over yet."

"What do you mean?" She waved to one of her aides and handed him her brief containing the evidence inventory. "He's guilty; they'll hang him for sure."

"No. He's got something up his sleeve. He's too smart to just admit his guilt and take his punishment," she said as she followed the prosecutor out. "The only reason we were able to catch him was because he got sloppy there at the last."

"You think he has a death wish?"

"No." They brushed past the reporters and their questions.

"My office will issue a prepared statement this evening," Haskins informed the press without missing a beat.

"You didn't see the way he looked at me while you were talking to the judge."

"No. I didn't." They stopped at the checking station where Marin retrieved her pistol. "What did he do?"

"He calmly smiled at me then winked." She shrugged as they stepped through the door of the elevator. "I think it's all a game to him. He wanted to get caught so he could see if the system could hold him. Intelligent murderers like him have done it before."

"And the system has held them," Haskins said matter-of-factly.

"Not always." The elevator car stopped at the ground level and opened its doors. "I think you should push for a quick execution."

"McCollum has already set the sentencing date. I can't change that. I will push for the court to forego the six-month waiting period before execution. I can evoke the Mount Rushmore act."

"How?" Marin felt for her keys as they neared the building's exit. "That has to do with terrorists." She thought of the three men she had seen shot two days after their trial for blowing George Washington's face off the famous mountain and killing twenty tourists in the process. "And that was fifty years ago."

"It's law." Haskins shrugged. "Rache can be viewed as an urban terrorist. Lord knows your team dredged up enough evidence to show his actions were all premeditated and designed to bring about public unrest, especially among the professional female population. The DA has also connected him with similar cases in New York City."

"Really? I hadn't heard that. Of course I've been pretty busy playing catch up since we closed this case."

"I'll bet you have." She stopped at a black sedan. "This is my car. Officer Schmidt, thank you for coming over. I'll see you in six weeks at the sentencing?"

She shook the other woman's hand. "I'm not sure. Something came up yesterday that is going to take the majority of my time."

"Another mystery?"

Marin sighed. "That's an understatement. It's going to be tough."

"I'm sure I'll read about it once you've cracked it."

"I'm sure you will."

"Well, thanks again for all your help. We'll do all we can to keep Rache on ice. I'll recommend isolation until the sentencing."

"Good idea." She turned and walked the short distance over to her little white car. It looked old and ragged compared to the one Haskins was getting into but, what should she expect on a county salary?

The drive back to Somerset County took about a half-hour. Traffic was unusually heavy for the midweek and she wondered if she had missed a holiday somewhere. She laughed at the thought. How could she have missed a holiday? She was only on call twenty-four hours a day, had ten murder investigations pending, the deal with Himmel Pharmaceuticals, her sister calling once a week, a mother over in Hunterdon County who was virtually an invalid and court appearances to make. Not a very full life.

She looked out the window as she neared the Somerset County Law Complex and saw the building where her church met. She could not even remember the last time she had been to a service.

The car nudged into its power port instinctively before she popped the door and hurried into her office. She found Kevin Neal waiting for her with a file pad and a list of questions.

"I know," she started before he could hit her with his verbal barrage. "He gave you how many?"

"Just three but they're all in Montgomery Township."

"Yeah, the three kids from Rocky Hill. That one's just a matter of finding a witness. Their Crime Busters program has a reward pending."

"Yes." He sat on the top of her desk, tapping the pad in an annoying manner. "But do you know how far that is to drive?"

"I don't see what difference that should make, Kevin. I'm just back from North Brunswick. It's all in the line of duty." She stopped and stared him off the desk. "If you wanted a local job, you should've applied with the Parking Patrol. Is there anything else?"

He moved toward the door. "I hear you're in with the Feds on something."

She clicked to the e-mail screen on her computer. "And if I am?" She glanced at his perfect little face, white teeth flashed at her. Not a hair was out of place. A Princeton graduate.

"If you need any help."

"You've got the help there in your hands."

He looked down at the pad. He had only been on the force for less than a year and was wanting to move up quickly. Like most of his peers, he was wanting to do it without working toward it. Marin did not like that about him. "This isn't what I meant."

"Well, I can talk to Hutchinson and see if he could give you that Peapack Boro case. Of course, I haven't had a chance to get by the coroner's to see the bodies yet."

His face lightened. They were not sure how many people had been murdered in the quiet northern suburb. Two for sure, maybe three. Whoever had done it had used some nasty explosives. "Uh, th-that far north?"

His inexperience could not be hidden.

She smiled. "Thanks for your help, Kevin." There was a message from McKinnon flashing urgently at her.

He gave her a terse smile and left the small room. She closed and locked the door behind him before opening the letter.

"I'm getting you some help," the agent's voice said as she initiated the recording. "He's pretty good with computers. He's one of the best the U.S. has working for them. He's with the Ulysses project at the moment, but I'm pretty sure I can sign him up. I'll call you when he comes back down."

She hit the erase command. "Comes back down?"

SIX

THE CONSTANT ROAR OF THE RAMJETS suddenly ceased. It had been in the background so long Mike hardly noticed it a few minutes after takeoff from Edwards. Now, it had been replaced by silence. He felt his body lighten as the ship changed attitude around him. His hand immediately went to the case in the seat beside him. The movement was difficult, as though his hand weighed twenty pounds.

He allowed himself a smile. They were still under thrust, only from rockets now. He had assumed the lack of sound had meant they would no longer be accelerating. Then he realized that outside the small window at his side there was no longer any atmosphere to carry the rumble of the motors. He felt the arm of his seat. It was still vibrating.

Through the view port the Earth's horizon bent slowly, rounding itself into the ball it would eventually become. He closed his eyes for a few minutes. By the time the ship reached Talinski's Station and Ulysses, the moon would be the dominant sphere in the eternal night sky of space.

He checked the case at his side again. Its battery lights continued to flash telling him the memory inside the module he would install on Ulysses was being maintained.

"We have achieved our lunar insertion orbit," the airplane turned spacecraft's captain informed him and the other technicians in the cabin. "Our escape burn is scheduled for zero nine twenty hours. That is roughly two minutes from now. If you will look to starboard you can see the east coast of the United States. New Jersey is directly above our wingtip."

Mike looked at the odd stretch of land as it rolled toward the ship's tail and met the ocean. He'd only been to New Jersey once or twice and did not really want to go back.

He adjusted his six-foot-one-inch frame in the seat again, making sure his head was facing forward before he closed his eyes. This was only his second trip to Ulysses and he still was not used to space flight. He reached up and aimed the air vent directly at his face as the burning feeling of motion sickness wrapped around the back of his neck and churned his stomach. He could not calculate their present velocity while his head was swimming, but he knew they had only left California less than twenty minutes ago and now New Jersey was far behind. If he looked again he could probably see the Pacific Ocean as they began their second orbit.

A solid thump and the crush of sudden acceleration pushed him back in his seat. He felt acid rise in the back of his throat as the ship reached toward its escape velocity and the moon.

He tried to clear his mind of the awful experience by thinking about Ulysses. He pictured her long, cylindrical form as it reflected sunlight against the hard blackness of the solar system. If it had been up to him he would not have named the probe after the ancient Greek leader who had been forced to roam the wilderness. He would have called her Mnemosyne, after the mother of the muses. After all, she represented memory and that was one thing Ulysses systems had. Memory.

Yet, Ulysses was a grand name that evoked heroism and adventure in the minds of the public and corporate sponsors. It commanded respect when the media reported on it. He doubted if half the public could even pronounce Mnemosyne.

The pressure of acceleration let up after a couple of minutes and he relaxed by taking in a deep, cool breath. In his mind's eye he saw Ulysses in its orbit above the limb of the moon.

Like a small insect caught in some great metallic web, she would ride to the edges of the solar system on the power of the sun using a magnetic sail.

The magsail was new to space flight. Alton Treon had introduced the world to his low cost superconductor only ten years ago. The superconducting coil was the key element in magnetic sail technology which involved a ring of charged material reacting against the solar plasma winds that constantly sped away from the center of the solar system.

Admittedly, the method of interplanetary flight was slow when compared to the forced accelerations a rocket could provide, but it was much faster than a conventional solar lightsail and more economical.

Since Ulysses' destination was interstellar space, she was also equipped with a N.E.R.V.A. rocket engine that would fire only when the solar winds were no longer useful as a means of propulsion. By that time Ulysses would be past Pluto's outermost orbit and approaching the realm of the comets.

Michael wished he was part of the vessel's compliment. To explore the stars was a lifelong dream of his and others on the Ulysses team. Reality told him it was not possible in this day and time but, perhaps one day the technology would grow to the point where star travel was more than science fiction. Until then, he conceded to himself, he would have to travel vicariously through his creation: the brain of Ulysses.

Michael Krumm was well known in his field. Many considered him to be the Mozart of software. He had been born with the ability to simply look at a problem and see it in its binary components and algorithms. By the time he had finished his secondary education he had been guaranteed a position with Worldsoft Technologies as a programmer.

Those were not fond days to remember. The corporation had a way of chewing its people up and spitting them out like gristle after all the good parts had been devoured. Fortunately, Michael saw it coming and got out before his brain was fried into non-creativity.

It was at that point when he found a position with the government. Not in computers but, working as a ranger and guide at Custer State Park in South Dakota. For five years he had given tours of the park and led sightseers to the largest American Bison herd in existence.

There among the dung and flies of the west he found contentment. It was a long way from everywhere; from Silicon Valley, from the small towns in Ohio where his life had began and a long way from the pressures of deadlines and doing the will of others. One day he promised himself he would return. His position as a ranger was being held open as part of his contract with the government.

During his time in the field he never abandoned his computer work. He became a very good model maker and did some freelancing for some of the big film companies and a few other concerns around the world. His full attention, however, remained with the park and it animals.

That is until Ulysses. Since then, the probe had been his life.

He felt he could thank Alton Treon, and his formulation of the superconductor for that. The man was obsessed with finding new ways the material could be used. He had invested his profits in everything from interstellar exploration to environmental reconditioning. His first atmosphere machine was being constructed on the fringes of Los Angeles, where it would reputedly clean the air like some great air conditioner.

He and NASA had personally sought Mike out for this job. Now, it seemed, it was coming to a close. In a matter of twelve hours he would install the final memory component in the huge, multi-exabyte computer he had designed. Shortly after that Ulysses would fire up its magnetic loop and ease out of its orbit.

He reached down and patted the case containing the two terabyte memory module. Suddenly sadness caught him by the throat. It was going to be like saying good-bye to a child knowing you would never see him again.

A bearded face bobbed down toward him. "There you go again." Tony Scavetta mocked his release of emotion. "You just gotta learn to let go of these things. It's just so much hardware."

Scavetta was the chief engineer on the project. He was the fifth man to hold the position since the project's inception. The others had left because of philosophical differences. Alton Treon was a hard man to get along with. Michael had managed to do so only because his personality was not prone to conflict. He always found a peaceful solution to any problem.

He looked at the case again. Its black cover glistened in the white cabin lights. He had chosen not to mark it with the usual fragility warnings. If it could not survive a simple shuttle trip to the moon it would never make it to Alpha Centauri.

"I don't think you'll ever understand, Tony."

"I know. I know." He sighed impatiently. "I've heard the 'like an artist,' 'this is my child' speeches before. You creative types are all alike."

Michael touched his own beardless face. It seemed strange not having any hair there anymore.

"How were you able to keep your beard? I thought regulations said we had to shave."

"They did." Scavetta rubbed his face. "But my name has a title in front of it. I'm a big chief, remember? I'm running this show for the next week."

Krumm laughed. "I did forget, but you make it easy to do so."

"What do you mean by that?"

"You're so down to earth, so normal. Not like the stuffed shirts that have worked on this project before you."

"Oh." He rubbed his head. "I'm not sure whether I've been insulted or not."

"I didn't intend any offense." He felt his face warm with embarrassment. "How long do we have until we dock?"

The engineer looked at his watch. "Mmm, I'd say twenty hours tops. Why?"

Michael shrugged. "It seemed like the proper question to ask."

"Hm." Scavetta moved into the seat across the aisle from the programmer. "So what is in that box you're carrying? I thought the whole system was already installed."

"I'm replacing the pilot."

"The pilot? Why?"

"I've been studying some of the old maritime sailors and their logs. I've basically written a program that will be able to analyze the solar winds like a yachtsman would the winds of the sea. Ulysses will be able to tack and steer herself in such a way as to get the most velocity out of the plasma stream. It should increase the vessel's efficiency twenty fold."

"That much? And how long did it take you to throw this little program together?"

"About two days. Why?"

The chief engineer smiled and shrugged. "That's why Treon and NASA hired you. It just blows my mind how you see things like that."

"It's a blessing and a curse." Michael allowed himself a chance to look out the small window again. Earth was now behind them out of his line of sight.

"I can see where it would be a blessing. You oughta be filthy, stinkin' rich by now. I'll bet you have Swiss bank accounts and everything."

He felt his the heat rise in his cheeks again. Anger washed against his normal spirit of self-control. His eyes narrowed. "What's this all about, Tony? My financial status is none of your affair. It has nothing to do with the system we've assembled."

Scavetta backed away slightly. "Hey, I'm just trying to make a little conversation. It's gonna be a long trip. Besides, this will be the last time the team is really together."

"I'm sorry," Krumm apologized, forcing a smile. His fair features lightened again complimenting his straight reddish-blonde hair. "I just like to keep my personal affairs personal."

"I see," the engineer conceded. "So, what's next for you? You going back to South Dakota or wherever it is you watch those buffalo?"

"Bison."

"Whatever. They're all just funny-looking cows."

"To the simple mind maybe. They are really quite majestic beasts. You know there used to be a time when a herd of them would run for miles? Thousands and thousands of them roamed the prairie freely."

"I know that story." Scavetta floated over into the seat facing Mike and strapped himself in. "All was perfect harmony until the white man came and destroyed the Native American paradise."

"That's the lecture. Only now it's returning to those times again. The park service has bought out a lot of the towns surrounding Custer, leveling them just so the herd would have a wider area to move about in."

"Ever been caught in a stampede of 'em?"

Michael grinned. "Once. I heard them coming though and had just enough time to clear out of my cabin. Actually, you feel them first." His gaze went distant as he returned to South Dakota in his mind. "You hear little things like plates buzzing against each other in the cabinets. Then the floor begins vibrating under your feet. When the chairs start rattling it's too late. They don't stop for anything. Not even a closed door."

"They busted your place up?"

"Oh, just the replaceable things. I've got a special steel coffin in the floor of my office in case I don't hear them. There's room enough in it for my CPUs and me, if an emergency arises. I keep my computer in there anyway because it's cool. My memory storage is in a vault in another part of the cabin."

"You still peck on the old virtual keyboard even when you're a ranger, huh?"

"I have to. Like I said, it's a blessing and a curse. If I don't do anything on it at least once a day, I develop something similar to a psychosis. I get very irritable and driven."

"Until you sit down and work on a program."

"Right. It's kind of like being an artist. If he can't produce art he is nothing. His life has no meaning."

"And your life has no meaning if you can't write programs."

"It's what I'm here for. It is my existence. It's how I bring order out of chaos."

"So, what is next for you? I've got some work lined up with AeroSys. They're doing something with the superconductor."

"Who isn't?" Michael said as he remembered the call that had reached him a half-hour before they launched. "I've got something simple lined up, then I suppose I'll head back out west."

"What's simple about programming?"

"The NBAC wants me to help them in an investigation. It'll probably involve some computer theft, maybe some reprogramming. I'm not really sure. It'll be light duty after the past few years."

"The NBAC?"

"National Bioethics Advisory Commission."

"Bioethics? Doctors?"

"No. It's more likely chemists and geneticists."

"Hm. Someone growing mutants?"

Michael shrugged. "It's never that grandiose. Probably some stolen information that has to be recovered. Maybe an experiment that has to be shut down. I'll find out more when I get back."

"Still with the Feds."

"Still with the Feds," Krumm smiled. "But in five more years I can retire comfortably."

"Right." The chief engineer laughed. "You will never retire."

Michael smiled back before looking at the black void

beyond the window again. "I hope you're right. I hope you are right."

"The blessing and curse again." Scavetta fidgeted with his seat straps. The conversation was over.

"Precisely."

"Well, nice talkin' to you. I'll see you at lunch."

"Sure. We'll need to go over some schematics before I install this. We'll talk again then."

"If not before." He looked at his watch again. "We've still got nineteen and a half hours of flight time in front of us."

SEVEN

GEOFFREY WALLRICH RAN A SWEATY PALM across his balding scalp. He was shaking, but he did not want anyone in the room to see. His hand rounded the back of his neck in a violent rub before grabbing the chair's arm. "Zwicknagl is coming here?"

"Yes," Kyle Pierce replied almost too coolly. "And she's going to want some answers that I can't give her. I thought you would appreciate a little warning."

"I do. I do, but how much warning are you giving me? When will she be here? I mean—I, we haven't broken into the system yet. We don't know how much is missing."

"Then I guess you had better see what you can do to correct that problem. That or bring in some boxes and get one of your cronies over there in research to help you pack. She's going to need a scapegoat if this thing gets out."

"I thought that was what you CEOs were for." He made a lame attempt at a joke. "I'm a working stiff. I actually get my hands on the research. Himmel needs me."

Pierce's dark features grew noticeably darker as he leaned forward on his elbows. "You're fortunate you don't answer directly to me Wallrich," he growled. "No one is irreplaceable."

"But we both answer directly to her." The researcher stood and moved toward the door. "It was Germany's idea we go along this path in the first place. They can't think I would take the blame for their project."

"Zwicknagl says she's coming over here to find out what her Americans are doing with her company. She also said something about rumors of illegal activity and a board of inquiry. A whole lot of nasty, official goings on that will eliminate certain corrupt elements within our reputable organization."

Wallrich could feel his stomach churning. "Only if this gets out."

Pierce nodded. "I would suggest you find your 'Bezalel' and then figure out some way to hide your little Genome Project before she arrives."

"When?"

Kyle Pierce allowed himself the luxury of producing a genuine smile. His dislike for Wallrich stemmed from years of noncooperation and the R&D unit's over inflated self-importance. "She'll be here on Wednesday, Doctor."

"Two days? Two days! I can't—" He found his mouth quivering as the words got lost somewhere between his brain and tongue. "She—"

"Well said." The CEO chuckled. "How many boxes will you need?"

Wallrich grabbed the doorknob and pulled. Two days. He did not notice Benton Stambaugh and his own chief of security as he stormed out of Pierce's office suite. In fact, he saw very little of anything as he made his headlong dash back to the haven of his building.

Pierce followed the chief of research and development as far as the double doors where he stopped and nodded to the two security officers. They both rose and followed him back into his ornate office.

Benton immediately found a chair to sit in making sure his hands were folded harmlessly in his lap. Pierce rarely had anything to do with him.

The other officer, Samuel Demonbreun, was less intimidated by the chief executive officer. His large, muscular frame loomed over both of the other men as he casually walked around the room looking at the different bobbles and artifacts Pierce kept on his shelves and cabinets. His black eyes seemed to be probing for anything out of sorts.

"Have a seat, Sam," Pierce ordered in his subtle manner.

Demonbreun moved slowly over to the leather chair beside Stambaugh. "You want him followed, sir?" he asked with narrowed eyes. "I can arrange it."

Pierce waved his hand in the air. "No. No. I don't believe we will have to worry about the good Doctor Wallrich. He'll bust his butt until he can gain access to the system. He just needs a little motivation sometimes."

"Then what are we here for, sir?" The security man rubbed the grip of his pistol unconsciously. "I have my people researching the records. We are doing our best to track down this guy from our end."

"Benton." The CEO ignored the R&D security man for the moment. "Miss Zwicknagl will be here on Wednesday. I need you to have this entire campus closed down to outsiders by the time she arrives. I also want double security on this building. I want her to get the impression that nothing could be removed from this facility without our knowledge and consent. Understood?"

"Certainly, sir." Stambaugh relaxed noticeably. "We'll make Fort Knox look like a Boy Scout camp."

"Right," Demonbreun snickered. "And we're to do the same with R&D. I find that insulting, sir. You know our security is the best in any industry. Its efficiency rating has doubled since I took over."

"I'm aware of that, Sam." Pierce sighed. The man was a self-proclaimed superguard and he did not mind letting others in on his little victories. "But that's not what I called you here for."

"What then?"

"You had a visitor the other day."

"Lieutenant Marin Schmidt of the Somerset County Sheriff's Department."

"Right."

"I've already begun a preliminary investigation of her. You want her followed?"

"What is it with you and following people?" Benton Stambaugh interrupted. "You're obsessive."

Demonbreun was unfazed by the outburst. "It'd pay for you to be a little obsessive yourself, fat boy."

"Gentlemen!" Pierce moved to his seat behind his desk in order to face them both. "You are both excellent security officers. I see no need in either of you copying the other. Now, shut up and let me give you your assignments."

"Yes, sir." Stambaugh lowered his head like a whipped puppy.

Demonbreun did not reply verbally. His black and challenging eyes met Pierce's.

"She will be back," the CEO continued, "and I want you to cooperate with her fully."

"What?"

"You heard me. Himmel is balancing on the precipice of dangerous international and political ground. If we are perceived as being overly covert in our actions toward the public authorities, it could mean a full-blown investigation into all of our activities. Am I understood?"

"Certainly," Benton replied.

"Sam?" Pierce drummed his fingers on the desktop. "This is not one of those war games you are so fond of engaging in. This is reality and it could mean the survival of this company."

The security chief raised his eyebrows. "You know about the militia?"

"I know a lot more about you than you ever dreamed possible, Samuel. I can reveal more if it's necessary."

"I don't think it is, sir." He managed a smile. "I'm impressed."

"Really?"

"Really, sir. I'm one of the best and you appear to have bested me."

Pierce rolled his eyes. Egomaniac. "Then this meeting is concluded. Gentlemen." He motioned toward the doors with his hand and watched them rise dutifully.

Before turning to go, Demonbreun stopped at the back of his chair. "I already know where she lives," he said confidently. "And I can get someone into her apartment if the need arises."

"You followed her already?" Stambaugh asked in protest. He remembered the detective very fondly. "You are a creep."

"I'm sure that won't be necessary," Kyle Pierce returned with a grin. "It is good to know though."

Benton Stambaugh shook his head. He did not like these power games. They were not his forte. Just simple, quiet security. That was his only concern. After all, they were in New Jersey.

Geoffrey Wallrich closed the door to his cluttered office and tried to find a chair to collapse in. The phone began buzzing as soon as he sat down.

"Wallrich!" he barked as soon as he found the unit.

The voice on the other end of the line belonged to Nancy Phin, the head of the research project that was giving him so much trouble. "Sir, are you all right?"

"No," he replied in a sigh. "And I'm about to get worse if we don't get into the mainframe."

Her voice changed from worried to one tinged with excitement. "That's what I wanted to tell you about. I brought Eric Auzins in."

"Eric Auzins? Who is he and why wasn't I notified he was coming over?"

"He's the head programmer at Northeast Net Systems. We

went to school together."

"Okay. Sorry. I should trust your judgment. He's already here?"

"That's all right, sir. I know how this must be affecting you."

Did she? He wondered. Did she know how his career was hanging in the balance over this one discrepancy, this one bumble? "Go ahead."

"Anyway," she continued. "I explained to him how we had been locked out of the system by our programmer before he quit. I told him it was an act of vengeance. He knows nothing about the project."

"Good." He began sorting through his calling cards looking for the one he had received nearly two years before from an agent of the National Center for Human Genome Research and the GenBank.

"He thinks he can get us in."

"How long?"

She hesitated. "It's all according to the trail, he says."

"Trail?"

"Yes. He told me all programmers have their own little idiosyncrasies. It's like a fingerprint. Once he figures that out he can proceed in breaking whatever coding is in place to keep us out."

"What kind of progress has he made so far?" A pile of cards slid forward from the back of his middle desk drawer.

Another long period of silence filled the air between them. "He's called up the models of the heart, liver and pancreas."

"Those are menu items, Nancy. Anyone who has ever sat down in front of a pad can bring those up."

"I know, sir." She sighed. "But he's the best I could find offhand. I suppose we have a deadline."

"Wednesday."

There was a strange sound, a sort of strangled laugh. "Pierce is that desperate?"

"Yes."

"Why?"

"Lynda Zwicknagl will be arriving on that day."

"Oh my god."

"Your god and every other god." He clapped his hand to his forehead. "If we can't get anything, any leads, anything at all, I'm afraid our research is toast. She wants answers."

"Of course. Uh, I'll see if Eric has any more associates that might be able to lend a hand. We'll go at this thing twenty-four hours a day."

"Okay, but be discreet. The more hands we have in the Petridish, the higher the probability of contamination."

"Understood. Wish us luck."

"For what good it will do, good luck." He broke the connection and pulled the stack of cards from the drawer. He stopped at one with the bold GenBank logo emblazoned across one corner. The name on it was Sterling Steeves: Memory Core Manager. He slid the card into his pants pocket for later use.

The phone buzzed again.

"Wallrich." His voice was calmer this time.

"Geoffrey?" The voice was a woman's. One he felt he should recognize, but had forgotten in the heat of his distress. "Geoffrey Wallrich?"

"Yes. Who's speaking please?"

"Marin Schmidt: Somerset County—"

"Oh yes." He interrupted. "The nice lady detective from the Sheriff's Department. How may I help you?"

Marin looked at the blank screen in front of her. She found it hard to believe he did not have a video connection. "Yes," she said cautiously. "The nice lady detective. Doctor, do you have a video hookup? I really feel strange talking to a voice only."

"I'm sorry," he responded. "If you remember the condition of my office, you know my situation."

"You have one, but you have no idea where it is." She rolled her eyes in disgust.

"Correct. Now, how may I help you?"

"I'm continuing my investigation into the theft of your—" What do you call something if you do not know what it is? "your information."

"The program. Yes. Yes." His voice trembled. If she had been in the room with him, she was certain his knuckles would be white and his hands would be shaking. "We have brought in some specialists to help us retrieve it. I think it would be a good idea if you came out here."

"That's what I was calling about. I would like to visit again and interview the team working on this project. Would tomorrow be all right?"

"No!" he blurted out as if he had just sat on a tack or the video transceiver for his phone.

"Well, how about Wednesday then?"

"No. Tomorrow's fine, if you can't come any sooner. Tonight would be better." His breathing became heavy then distant again. "Yes, tonight. Come tonight if at all possible. We need to solve this deal quickly. Come tonight. Security will be expecting you."

"I still have my badge," she informed him. "Doctor?"

The speaker hissed with dead air.

Marin looked at her watch. It was nearly time to go home, peel off her gun and relax. Five o'clock. If Wallrich had not been so blasted overly cooperative she could see herself doing just that.

She rubbed her head and cursed her dedication to duty. She had to go out there now. The door was wide open. It would be a mistake not to take advantage of it.

Maybe this time she could find out exactly what it was she was supposed to be looking for.

EIGHT

BY THE TIME SHE MADE it out to Himmel it was fast approaching nine o'clock. She had stopped for a bite to eat and a call to McKinnon. He was not much help, requesting only that she not let Wallrich know she knew anything about the company's reputed crime against the Genome Project. It would be difficult to hide her new knowledge about Himmel, but she felt she could use it in an educated manner.

A new security man met her at the gate and insisted on riding into the R&D compound with her. She got his name, Sam Demonbreun, and managed to ask him a few questions about the research going on within the facility. He assured her he knew very little about what went on inside the building's labs, but he did know the movements of every person on the grounds. No one could have broken into the building and stolen anything without his permission or knowledge.

"So I can put you on my suspect list then?" Marin had remarked half jokingly.

His eyes narrowed in a way that sent chills up her spine. "I'd never betray an employer, Officer Schmidt. Never," he growled.

She tried to shake the confrontation off. "I'll quote you on that."

"That would be wise." He stepped out of the car and opened the blue door for her. "Doctor Wallrich will be right down."

"Thank you." She smiled and placed her pad back in her pocket.

The corridor seemed much brighter than it had the other day. Of course then she had entered it from a beautiful, light spring afternoon. The heavy darkness outside had changed her perspective on the building.

It still looked like a stainless steel fortress when she had approached it. The moon cast a silvery edge to the structure accentuating its bleakness and hard edges. She had seen movement behind heavily tinted glass windows, but movement that could be taken for fluttering curtains more than busy humans.

The sound of hard soled shoes against tile alerted her to Wallrich's approach. She could see his face was drawn with concern. The diplomatic smile of their last meeting had been lost somewhere.

"Doctor Wallrich." She moved toward him.

He extended a hand. "Glad you could come so soon. I'll take you to the lab."

She tried to make light of his mood in order to get him talking. "No sense in beating around the bush."

"No. No sense in it," he grumbled as they made their way toward the double security doors at the hallway's end. Red probing eyes scanned them from high corners before unlocking and opening the doors. "But that's all we're doing."

"Beating around the bush?"

"Yes. I knew we shouldn't have committed ourselves to such an outlandish undertaking, but Germany insisted. It's not my fault. I'm just an administrator. Do you understand that? My job was simply to put the proper people in place to perform the job."

Marin stopped. "Doctor, I'm not quite following you."

"Yes, you are," he snapped at her. "How else will you find the lab? I've assembled the whole team. You should have plenty of resources to piece together exactly what took place and find Bezalel. You can do it tonight, can't you?"

"Hold it." She stopped. "I was called in on this case to find a culprit. The other day, you told me nothing had been stolen. Your only problem was denial of access to a project you were developing."

"Right. We still can't get into the computer and we still don't know where Bezalel is. I suspect a keen detective mind like yours will be able to figure out a way to do just that. It should be much easier than following a vague trail of dead bodies.

"By the way, I heard he pleaded guilty."

"Yes, he did." She began walking again, only because he had. "And yes I can solve this thing, but not overnight. There are certain lines I will have to take. There's a recipe I use to decipher facts. The important thing is it takes time."

"Time is something I do not have, Officer Schmidt. The chairman of the board will be arriving in just under thirty-six hours. If I don't have an answer for her by then, I'm history."

"I understand now." She stopped again, crossing her arms in disgust. "You're using me and my department to fix your problem. You could care less if I solved this thing beyond a shadow of a doubt. You just want me to save your butt and probably Pierce's too."

"I could care less about Pierce," he barked.

"That's not the point. I'm committed to this case, Doctor, but not for your well-being. A crime has taken place. My job is to find the perpetrator and see that he or she pays their debt to society and your company for the damage that has been rendered. I will be objective and I will require more time than thirty-six hours. If that does not suit you, that's tough."

Wallrich placed his hands on his hips and began to mouth something. He stopped himself, raised his right hand to point out something then stopped again.

"Spit it out, Doctor. We're wasting time."

He finally shoved his hands in his lab coat pockets and

stomped off down the corridor. She followed.

The "lab" was not what she had expected to see. It wasn't a room full of glass piping stacked on black slate worktables and Bunsen burners with white-coated researchers plying diligently away at unlocking the biomolecular secrets of the universe. Instead it was a brightly lit cavernous expanse filled from one end to the other with maroon modular computer memory towers. The hum of the drives sounded like a swarm of angry insects as they churned away at the information hidden within their magnetically coded discs. She stopped and searched for a break in the rows, a place where a human could find separation from the megalithic assemblage.

Wallrich disappeared down a yellow-marked aisle that ran toward the geographic center of the room. There, just above the tower tops, she could barely make out a glassed in cage. She could see the busy shapes of people hovering around the room's center.

"Are you coming or not, Lieutenant?" The doctor snapped as he reappeared.

"What are you doing with all this hardware?"

"We needed a few terabytes of memory for this project." He waved his hands in an attempt to encompass the whole room. "These towers are all outdated now. They have been for years, but we couldn't afford to keep up with technology after the superconductor units were first manufactured."

"Yes, but for what?"

He started walking toward the control room again. "All will be revealed if you will come with me."

They marched through the small artificial canyon that led to the elevated glass enclosure. Once there they took the mauve carpeted steps up to the working level. She was surprised to see such attention to aesthetic detail in a work area. The handrail she slid her hand along was polished oak balanced on ebony supports. A few nondescript prints hung at eye level in the control room foyer. They were just splashes of color put there to relieve the strained eyes of screen watchers as they left their posts. Interior designers did much the same thing with hospitals and elevators. They had for over a century.

A tall brown-haired woman met them as they entered. Her features were exaggerated; high cheekbones, small teeth, gummy smile and soft, solemn green eyes. Her hair fell to her shoulders, the curl that had been there at the start of the day had relaxed into gentle waves that rolled onto tired shoulders.

Wallrich introduced her in a perfunctory manner. "Marin Schmidt, meet Nancy Phin, project director."

The other woman's hand was surprisingly warm and dry as Marin took it in hers. "I'm with the Sheriff's Department," she completed her introduction.

"I'd heard Pierce had called the law in." Phin took her hand back and placed it in her other one behind her back. "I disagreed."

"Why?"

The researcher shrugged. "What can you do that we can't?"

"That's a good question, but moot."

"Moot?" Phin loomed over her. "To what degree? We have one of the most powerful computer systems in the nation surrounding us."

"Yes, you do," Marin smiled as she looked at the expanse of towers radiating from all sides of the control complex. "And as I understand it, you can't get into it. Hence, it has been stolen from you."

Nancy Phin's face reddened. "We can get into it."

"But not the part you want," she grinned and stepped further into the room. "I can't get into it either, but perhaps I can help you find the man or woman who locked you out of it. That's my job. I find people."

"I see," the other woman conceded.

"She's pretty good at it too," Wallrich added. "I think that's why our esteemed CEO let our problem slip into the hands of the sheriff."

Phin huffed. "Well, I suppose you will be wanting access to records and my staff."

"Yes. I would like to interview anyone who has dealt directly with the stolen material, anyone who might have had contact with this Bezalel character."

Wallrich nodded his head in approval. "Thirty-six hours, Nancy. That's all we've got."

The project director pursed her lips and pinched them with her fingers, her brow knit into furrows of concentration. "None of us had direct contact with the programmer. We simply checked his," she stopped self-consciously, "or her, progress."

"Daily?" Marin pulled her trusty notepad out.

"Sometimes hourly. You wouldn't believe how fast this person could work at times."

"What was the programmer doing?"

Phin walked over to a blank computer screen. "It would be best if I showed you." Her hand flew deftly over the slim controls at the screen's base until a three-dimensional picture formed of a beating heart.

Marin walked over to take a closer look at the form. It looked like a real heart. The surface was slick with membrane and quivering with life. "Your programmer did this?"

"Yes. Well, he set in place a program that allowed us to build this particular organ."

"To build it. From what?"

"Tell her, Nancy." Wallrich's voice was strained. He did not want the detective to know what they had done, but there was no way around it.

"We have before us a virtual heart."

"A virtual heart," Marin repeated. "A computer's representation of a heart."

"No," Phin corrected. "It is a working model of the actual organ. Right now I could call up virtual scalpels and incise it. If I did, you would see blood seep from the openings and layers of muscle. Inside of it are chambers that pump virtual blood through hidden arteries."

"So, it's a real heart?"

"Within the parameters of this particular program."

"How? I mean, are there virtual cells inside the virtual muscle? Are they being fed virtual oxygen from virtual lungs somewhere?"

"I think you're beginning to see the whole picture." Wallrich patted her on the shoulder.

"How?" Marin rubbed her forehead. "Just a minute. Let me think."

Nancy Phin looked over her shoulder toward the frantic programmer she had invited in. He remained hunched over the screen, still unsuccessful.

"How was this programmer able to do this? It would take an incredible amount of information to build a model of even a single cell."

"Precisely." Phin spun back around. "And within our system we have that information. Have you ever heard of the Human Genome Project?"

Marin tried her best to look vaguely informed. "Yes. That was the project to map all the genes in the human body."

"You have heard of it then. You know it was successfully completed?"

"Well—"

"And in its secondary phase the molecular structure of each gene was plotted out in each strand of DNA. From there, each gene's function was determined." Phin's eyes widened to the point where she resembled a madwoman. "And from that point the building blocks of the human body were cataloged and decoded."

"And now," Wallrich chimed in, "we know which genes determine the growth and function of every part of the human body."

Marin felt her stomach churn as an uneasy feeling darted back and forth across the base of her brain making her neck burn. It was fear, pure and simple. The two researchers had the basic knowledge available to alter a human being. Thoughts of mutant monsters rose up from the creative recesses of her mind. Superhumans, genetically engineered to rule, Subhumans, built as worker drones. Science fiction becoming reality.

"My god," she whispered as her features twisted with concern.

Wallrich shook his head. "I know what you're thinking, Lieutenant. And no, it's not all that simple. There are still decades of experimentation in front of us before we become the mad scientists the world fears."

"That's your goal?"

Phin laughed out loud. It was a high, nasal cackle, witch-like and haunting. The whole situation was becoming too weird. "You think for a moment a company like Himmel would invest in something so threatening. No, Officer Schmidt. It's too politically precarious. We intend only to use the information we have to help find cures for hereditary diseases and environmental mutations. The world is safe."

"For now," Marin countered. "But how long will it be before such things happen?"

"A long time." Wallrich folded his hands in front of him, fig leaf pose. "Hang around here. Roam our facilities and you will see research is a slow and tedious task."

"It's been more than a century since the Genome Project was first conceived and we are only to the point of understanding each nucleotide's function. There are still finite sequencing discrepancies we have no answers to. You should not fear the geneticists."

Marin's attention turned back to the throbbing heart encased in the computer screen. "Yeah, but you've been able to do that."

"It's virtual," Phin smiled, her hand patting the picture affectionately. "It's a construct from the information we have available to us."

"And you could use it to experiment, to create mutations." She frowned and looked directly at Wallrich. "It seems as if there should be something unethical about that."

"It's a computer model." Wallrich knew what she was leading up to, or so he thought. "It's no worse than creating a virtual city and then setting off a twenty-megaton bomb in one of the buildings to see what the damage would be. The program will give you physical damage results along with those of the dead and wounded. No one will be hurt, but a great deal can be learned."

"That is what we intend to do, what we are doing here." Nancy Phin's voice filled with excitement and compassion. "We are using these models to measure the effects of model drugs and genetic alterations. Always with the public's health and well-being in mind."

A stream of incoherent expletives rose from the other side of the room where the crowd was. Nancy moved in that direction. Marin and Wallrich followed.

"What is it?" Phin asked the middle-aged man behind the keyboard.

He turned away from the screen. His bloodshot eyes looked directly into the director's face. Marin thought she could see tears welling up at their edges. "I can't get in. I've tried everything in the book." His voice choked with defeat. "I'm sorry, Nancy, but this guy is good. Real good. There are no less than twenty-seven different paths into your program and twenty-seven coded lockouts for each path. Together they make a fractal equation that has to be resolved. It'd take me a year to just figure one out. I'm sorry."

He looked at the staff around him. "This is humiliating."

Phin put a firm hand on his shoulder. "Thanks, Eric." Then she turned to Marin. "Well, Officer, I guess that leaves it all up to you. We can't get to it without Bezalel."

"And we can't get Bezalel without you," Geoffrey Wallrich snickered.

Marin did not respond immediately. Instead she stared at the columns of data rolling and rolling up the screen the programmer had just abandoned. Her eyes narrowed as she put together the information she had just seen. Computer models of organs based on genetic maps.

They still had those.

Then what could be in there? What could be so important?

"What did he build for you?" she finally asked.

Phin's mouth opened then closed again.

Wallrich leaned over and put his mouth to her ear. His breath was hot and the whisper was barely audible.

She jerked her head away as if his lips were made of molten iron.

Had he said, "A man"?

NINE

A THOUSAND DISTORTED SUNS BOUNCED THEIR light off the wrinkled covering of the mirror pure foil insulation protecting Ulysses' outer skin. The myriad lights created a sparkly, fairy world pattern on the belly of the small worker pod as it maintained a safe distance from the probe.

Michael moved carefully away from the small craft and waved to its pilot as he cleared the webbing that protected the launch frame from possible mishaps, like pods that could not slow in time. Once inside the flimsy shell, he used the web to stabilize his own erratic approach. He set his feet toward the maintenance hatch and pushed off. His breathing echoed around the small helmet, throbbing through his ears.

Ulysses loomed before him as he made his descent. It floated above him like a great cylindrical tower. A monument to its creators.

All along the probe's hull blisters of instrument clusters rose like great welts from some unknown space disease. He knew there were over three hundred such clusters all around the vessel. And for each cluster there was a CPU carefully watching the readings from each sensor. Each CPU in turn had two backups watching over it.

Michael sighed as he reached the hatch. It had been a long ordeal designing a computer system this sophisticated. He had no doubt as to its functionality. After all, it was his design, his computer programs watched over every inch of the probe. If it failed there would be no one else to blame.

The hatch opened easily after he keyed in his access code. He pulled it to the side allowing it to rest weightlessly on its hinges. The module he had carried by his side all the way from Earth now slid through the opening before him. He made sure a hand was on it at all times, even as he switched the work lights on.

Inside the trunk of the great behemoth, a thousand similar modules towered away from him toward the spacecraft's nose. To a layman, or saboteur, it would be a confusing sight. Each CPU looked exactly the same. The only way to know which was used for what function was to either be the system's designer or have a very good map.

Michael did not need the map. He felt great pride well up in his chest as he pushed off toward the higher speed calculations section. It was there that the new module would be replaced. Once locked in, the system would then come fully to life.

It only took a few minutes to reach the proper level.

The programmer reached out and grabbed a maintenance rung to stop himself. Deft hands removed the plastic cover over the female port. He let it float free behind him before opening the case. The chrome module floated free of its foam packing and extended its locking clamps.

Michael touched a button in the center of the male pins. He stopped. Why call them pins? They were more like spikes.

The unit hummed to life as he guided it into place. Small sensors on the ends of the clamps told the unit to grab its opposites on the system housing while small motors pulled the shiny box home.

Michael felt it lock into place.

A cold sweat broke out on his forehead, surprising him. He had not expected to react that way. His heart rate increased for a few minutes as he floated free, staring at Ulysses' guts as she came to life.

"You okay in there, sir?" the distant pilot inquired. "You're not having any trouble, are you? Your heart rate's up to one twenty."

"I'm fine." He tried to sound calmer than he actually was. "Adrenaline rush."

"Ah." The pilot chuckled back. "Understood."

He felt his face warm with embarrassment. As closely as his activities were monitored out here he would have to be careful what he did or said. It was not because of corporate or governmental paranoia, he knew, but for the overall safety of anyone working in this environment where the least little accident could lead to instant death.

Suddenly, he realized how fragile his situation was. Surrounded by plastic and polymer filaments, his own life was inches away from termination. The pack that maintained his air, the suit that held the proper pressure against his skin, the bubble over his head that blocked ultraviolet light and harmful gamma rays, all kept him alive in the uninhabitable world of space.

It was not uninhabitable. That was a fallacy. No. Mankind, with all its ingenuity had managed once again to place its existence in a world where it did not belong. The species would spread out too, now that the financial barriers, that had held its expansion into the cosmos in check for so long, were finally dissipating.

Michael knew the world had Alton Treon to thank for this new revolution. His superconducting material had opened doors that seemed forever shut, or at least extremely expensive to open. At this moment the engineering and scientific community were rewriting the boundaries of mankind's technology. It was an event being compared to the computer revolution of the previous century. He was not sure it was all that significant, but he was a little prejudiced in his opinion where the computer revolution was concerned. To him it was a continuing growth. The superconductor was merely an invaluable tool in the latest propagation of artificial intelligence technology.

He moved down the line of computer modules to the test center. It flashed for his proper ID to be used. He touched the pad on his left arm and pulled the hookup from its pocket below the pad. The leader snapped into place without a sound. A simple touch on the "enter" button caused the machine's screen to roll to life. Binary words and pictures scrolled past his view as he watched. He could read most of what the CPU was telling itself, initiate this subsystem, checking such and such software, verifying all enabled functions, and the like. A picture of Earth, a man, a woman, a map of the solar system, of the galaxy, with an approximate location guide flashed by.

"Okay," he said as he tapped in an alternate command which would move him beyond the start-up level. Ulysses would continue to initiate its systems as he moved to what he liked to call the higher brain functions.

"Working," the vessel acknowledged him through his headset.

"Is that Ulysses?" the eavesdropping pilot asked.

"Yes. She's finally awake," Michael commented as he entered more commands.

"Up time. Twenty-two seconds," the male-like voice reported from the probe's bowels. "Twenty-three seconds."

"Discontinue up count," the programmer ordered. "Report launch readiness."

The computer went silent for a moment. Michael imagined he could see lines of power coursing through the massive system as each sensor, each backup and communications with both the space station and ground stations was tested. If this had been a motion picture, perhaps like one of those old Spielberg flicks, he thought, there would be a foggy blue light gliding up and down the tunnel-like interior of the vessel. But that was fiction, wasn't it? Light and computers were not so dramatic. They did not care about impressing the humans around them, entertaining them. They were purely functional.

"Up time: Four minutes, ten seconds. System functioning at optimal levels. Launch sequence primed."

"Initiate at command from JPL. Code JPL two two alpha."

"Waiting," Ulysses bellowed. Was that anticipation behind the artificial voice?

It could be. Michael knew his system was one of the largest computer networks ever assembled in human space. He knew it was the largest ever sent out of the solar system.

"That's it," he told both the pilot and Ulysses. "Phase two," he added, "will be enabled by code E.X. three one colon two three."

"Waiting," Ulysses replied again.

"Phase two?" the nosy pilot inquired.

"Post launch." Michael hoped the minor irritation in his voice could be heard by his escort. He was not in the mood to be drilled about the program.

"Gotcha!" the pilot said. What he had gotten Michael was not sure.

"I'm on my way out." He patted the test center gently and unsnapped his suit cable then resealed it in its pocket. "Godspeed," he finished to his computers.

If they replied, he did not hear them.

Talinski's Station was a modest space platform assembled from loose rocket housings, girders and the occasional specialty module. It was not much unlike the old space station Freedom NASA had attempted to build in the latter part of the previous century.

But unlike that endeavor, Talinski's was a privately funded construct built in 2059 by a Russian businessman who had grown tired of seeing his country bested by the international programs.

Michael had the honor of staying in the Talinski Hub, the central part of the station built exclusively for Talinski. Its ornately decorated rooms reminded him of sections of old Czarist mansions he had seen in museums. Religious icons were placed reverently in key sections of the wall space accentuated by the red velvety floral patterned, gold leaf wall paper. Of course the disciplines of free fall ruined the total ambiance of the Hub. Resting straps were placed along the "ceiling" and along sections of wall. The bedroom consisted of a coffin-like device shoved unobtrusively into a darkened corner. The bar floated freely next to the foyer, fastened to the doorframe by a golden rod. What would Russian territory be without its Vodka?

The modern things were molded in high impact, multicolored plastic. An interior decorator would have had a stroke. Nothing here was very well coordinated.

Michael laughed to himself as he took in the surroundings. Wasn't that the premise behind Talinski's declaration? After all the station was made up of what had been discarded over the past century of space travel. Why not have the interior be a similar cacophony of style and functionality?

He floated over to the room's one view port and stared out at the crescent Earth. In a short time he would be back under her influence. In a way he dreaded returning. It wasn't so much the return as much as he dreaded the starting over. This pending project with the NBAC smacked of complicated bureaucratic undercurrents that could lead to years in court, especially if his suspicions were true.

It was not a simple matter of exploration like Ulysses. This had to do with underhanded acquisitions and manipulation of data. It was corporate America through and through.

The communication panel next to the coffin buzzed.

"Yes?" He allowed himself to float closer to the sleep area.

"You all set?" The voice was Tony Scavetta's.

"Ready," he answered as he lifted the thin Velcro-edged sheet that would hold him through his sleep period. "Is the N.E.R.V.A. on line?"

"Look out your window, if you can. She'll be doing a

couple of test bursts about now. Ulysses is leaving the docking cradle."

Michael reoriented himself and floated back toward the porthole. At the edge of his view he could just make out the blue flares from the probe's engines. Soon the Magsail coils would begin charging.

"Anywhere on the station we can get a better view?" he asked the engineer.

"Sure," Scavetta laughed. "But you'll have to suit up again."

"That's no problem. I didn't come this far to miss it."

"Okay. I'll send someone over for you."

In a few minutes a hollow knocking sounded at his door. He opened it to see a beautiful young woman, maybe in her mid-twenties. She smiled revealing perfect white teeth. Her short cropped blonde hair labeled her as a worker, but she could have easily been an administrator or a public relations officer. He was surprised at how his heart raced when he looked into her aqua blue eyes. He'd been behind the old virtual keyboard too long.

"Hi!" she beamed. "You must be Michael Krumm."

"I most certainly am." He smiled back.

She held onto the doorframe and extended a delicate hand. "Cheryl Caenier."

"Mmm. French?"

"North American. My maiden name's Hulett."

"Oh." Michael felt his heart slow suddenly and heavily. So much for the hormone rush. "Your husband works here?" he asked politely, affording the distance holy matrimony deserved.

"Yes." She flushed. "He's the vice-administrator. I'm a sub-engineer. I've done some time on your project."

Michael shrugged. "It's not really mine. Alton—"

"I know. Treon owns it, but your brains built it." She turned and began down the polished steel corridor that led away from his suite. "Tony Scavetta says you're a blasted genius. I believe him. I have never seen a system as complex as Ulysses. We had quite a bit of difficulty assembling that monster. Many twenty hours days went into that son—"

"How long have you been up here?" He interrupted. Talking about his work made him uncomfortable. Like any artist he could accept a generalized praise session, but when it came to picking at the piece, it was better to move on.

"This stint?" She bit her lower lip as they reached a tube that would take them into one of the "upper" modules where Scavetta was waiting for them. "I think it's been six—no, seven months."

"You're about due for an Earthside vacation then." He watched her carefully as she worked her way up the ladder in front of him.

"Nah!" she laughed. "Nothing there I want to see. We've got a centrifuge. I work out regularly."

He smiled. "It shows."

"Excuse me?"

It was his turn to flush with embarrassment. "I'm sorry."

She stopped. "Quite all right." Her head bent so their eyes met. "You don't look so bad yourself. My husband is away at Copernicus for the rest of the week. Could I—"

Michael stopped her mid-sentence. "Oh no, ma'am. I was just making an observation. I'm sorry if I insinuated that I—"

"You would want to, wouldn't you?"

"Yes, but wanting and doing are two completely different matters." He felt himself drift back a few paces. "Thanks anyway."

"It's because I'm married, isn't it?"

"That would be the main reason. Yes."

She looked away then looked back. "You'd honor such a bond?"

"Of course. Yes. It's wrong to commit adultery."

Then she pulled herself on. "A man with morals. How quaint."

Mike did not know how to answer her. He wasn't sure if she

had just put him down or was really amazed by his convictions. Spacers were a completely different society. He guessed it came from the constant presence of instant death. It made them grab life more forcefully. Any part of life. He was sure her husband would not have minded the infringement, but it just was not right.

Tony met him at the top of the ladder. His eyes lingered on Cheryl just long enough for her to notice then he turned and smiled at Krumm. "I see you've met the vice-administrator's wife."

Michael nodded. "Where's that view you promised?"

He pointed to a room full of space suits. "Through this door. I'm sure there's a suit that will fit." He looked at his watch. "We've got about twelve minutes. Ulysses is still jockeying for free space."

Michael imagined he could see blue flashes through a small porthole near the door. It took a lot of maneuvering to get a ship the size of Ulysses out of the cradle. He found a bright orange suit near the end of the rack and slipped into it. Its skin-tight material gripped his body like rubber as he fought to pull the unit over his coveralls.

As he snuggled the helmet into its collar ring he heard Scavetta's voice talking to someone else. "He's over there. We were just getting ready to do an E.V.A."

"Mister Michael Krumm?" a young, stern voice asked as he felt the flat of a hand touching his shoulder.

"Yes." He fought to remove his helmet. Then, once it was off. "I'm Michael Krumm."

"ID please." The black uniformed man held out his hand.

Michael rolled his eyes and unzipped the suit so he could reach into his coveralls' breast pocket. He pulled the plastic card out and showed it to the man.

"Very good." He turned toward the door. "Come with me please."

"Why?" He remained in place. "We were just getting ready

to watch our project launch."

"That will have to wait, sir," the man said nonchalantly.

"It can't." He heard his voice whine and looked at Cheryl with a touch of embarrassment. He wanted to see his ship go.

"He's right." Tony Scavetta interrupted. "What could be so important?"

"You will not keep the President waiting, Mister Krumm. His schedule is much more important than yours."

"Treon?" Mike sighed. "He'll understand."

"No, sir. The President of the United States. He wants to talk to you immediately."

TEN

MARIN HANDED HER CARD TO THE guard at the east gate and waited until her credentials had cleared. She looked around at the shaded area with its wrought iron fences, perfectly sculpted bushes, perennial flowerbeds, well-groomed lawn and multiple rows of barricades. Never in her life had she thought she would get the chance to visit the nation's capital on official business; let alone the White House.

"Okay, ma'am," the voice at the end of the stiff blue uniformed arm said as it returned her ID to her. "Mister McKinnon will be waiting for you on the porch. Welcome to Washington, D.C."

"Thank you." She took her card back and slipped it into her pocket, adjusted her jacket and moved through the gate. Somehow she felt strangely underdressed. She wasn't sure if it was because she was walking into the White House or the fact she had left her pistol behind. Its uncomfortable presence under her arm left that ghost of a feeling. She guessed it was how an amputee felt when remembering a lost limb.

McKinnon saw her and jogged down the drive to meet her. "I see you didn't have any trouble finding the place."

She gave him a smirky grin. "Was that a joke?"

He shrugged, ignoring the slight. "After you called me I saw no reason why we shouldn't bring this to the top immediately. I'm glad you could come down on such short notice. The

President is very anxious about this thing."

"I imagine so. It was the ethics issue that got him elected." Though on the negative side.

He was all for experimentation with the human body. Many of the states agreed with him and the general population did not know or care enough to stop him. Ignorance or apathy? We don't know and we don't care.

"Yes, and if you got the straight story from Wallrich, Himmel has something he wants very badly."

"Something that he can't get." She remembered the frustrated computer programmer. "Himmel can't even get it. They're locked out."

"I know that, but they don't have Michael Krumm."

"Who?"

"He's the computer jock I told you would be joining us. He's the best there is."

"How come I've never heard of him?"

McKinnon shrugged again as he opened the door for her. "Maybe you don't ever watch the news. He's the chief programmer for Ulysses. Fair-haired guy, bearded."

She remembered the face she had seen the first day of the investigation, before she had been called back into the office to meet McKinnon for the first time. "Okay. Soft-spoken fellow."

"That's him." They passed another security checkpoint. "We've arranged a conference call with him. He's on his way back from the moon at this moment."

"So, what's the President want to do with Himmel's program?"

McKinnon flushed for the first time since she had met him. "I think I'll let him tell you."

They entered the ancient building. Marin's first impression was of a musty museum. She could not escape the smell of old decaying plaster walls, the lumber buried underneath and the antiquities scattered throughout the building. She realized she was not far from the truth. The White House was a museum.

She had learned in elementary school that one time it had been open to the public. Daily tours were given to the citizens of the United States. After all it was their White House. The castle the people had built for their temporary king.

She also knew all that had stopped a few short years before her birth. That was when a few well packed men had charged through the lines of tourists and stormed the building. Each one detonating a suicide bomb as he got as far as he could into the White House.

Their mission was successful. They had killed President Julie Ann McCord, the nation's first woman president.

They had called themselves "Men for the Common Cause," which meant nothing until you delved deeper into their group's history. It was one of the many extreme right-wing organizations that McCord's Vice President, Thomas Korrigan, granted asylum within the bounds of the newly formed theocracy of Utah. In fact, that event was the beginning of the founding of the right-wing's haven of states now known as the Co-Federation of Believers.

It took a constitutional reform only three years to pass public scrutiny to allow the formation of this federation within the bounds of the federal government of the United States. All right-wing extremists had been encouraged to migrate to the established states and they had.

Utah, Nebraska and New Mexico still had representation in Congress, but like other United States territories, they no longer had voting rights. Their borders were also watched extremely closely by the nation's military.

It had been the beginning of the disintegration of the once proud united nation of states.

They walked down a sparsely decorated hallway and into a suite of tiny offices. McKinnon opened the door to one small room marked "Conference" and offered her a chair next to a plain pressboard table, laminated to look like rich cherry. The illusion would have been successful if not for the rings of coffee stains that had lifted the paper covering free of its base and the many chips knocked away from its edges by chairs like hers.

In the table's center stood a phone picture cube. Its quad divided screens announced that the system was waiting.

"Something to drink?" the Bioethics agent offered.

"No." Marin adjusted her jacket. The room seemed stuffy to her. "I'm fine. When will the President get here?"

McKinnon chuckled. "He'll be joining us on the conference call. He never comes down here."

"Oh." She put her hands on the dirty tabletop. "Why did I even have to come to Washington? We could have done this from any office."

"Yes." The agent grabbed a cup of coffee from a tiny dispenser near the door. "But any office doesn't have a secure channel like the White House. This thing has become a matter of national security."

She found herself frowning. "You Feds are overly paranoid, aren't you? It's just a stupid computer model."

"Oh no, Officer Schmidt." His eyes widened greedily. "It's much more than that. Much more."

He punched in a sequence on the pad next to the box.

"Yes?" a deep male voice answered.

"This is Agent Douglas McKinnon. You can tell the President we're ready anytime he is."

Marin felt her heart skip a beat. Even though she was in the equivalent of the White House's root cellar, she could not escape the excitement of thinking she was actually going to be talking to the President of the United States of America.

It didn't matter that the country he was running was falling apart at the seams. It didn't matter that his powers had been cut by a greedy Congress, Senate and Supreme Court so many times he was merely a figurehead. He was the President and those who did not hate him owed him reverence. It was simply a matter of historic tradition.

He was the one man in the U.S. who could only be accessed when he wanted to be. She stopped and corrected the thought. He was the only public figure who enjoyed that kind of security. And why not? Every presidential assassination had been a tough morale blaster for the nation to overcome.

The phone beeped and McKinnon opened the line.

Not a hair rested out of place on President Lansing T. Gates' head. Perfectly sculpted features stared into the receiver on his desk. He surveyed McKinnon and Marin with deep blue eyes finally offering them a perfect smile. Spokesman for the government to the people and rich beyond his needs. Old computer money.

"M-Mister President." McKinnon surprised her by the slight stammer. "May I present Officer Marin Schmidt of the Somerset County Sheriff's Department, New Jersey."

"Mister President." She nodded.

"Pleased to meet you, Sharon."

"Marin, sir."

"Yes." He smiled again. His voice was announcer perfect. He was the ultimate public official. "Marin."

"Thank you, sir."

"Before we call on our astronaut computer programmer, I'd like to ask you a few questions. You seem to have stumbled onto quite a find. Do you have any idea what the implications are to this, what shall we call it, this virtual human being?"

"Other than the obvious medical applications, no, sir."

"I thought so. Now, Agent McKinnon, you have told me that this man is perfectly human?"

"Well, sir. My statements are simply conjecture. No one has seen him yet. Himmel can't gain access to the program."

"But if we could talk to him, he would seem normal."

"Sure. Only he's inside the computer."

Gates smiled. "Wonderful. That would make him impervious to any outside influence, such as military."

"I can't say, sir."

"Here's what I'm driving at. If it has been assembled from genetic information for the average human, with all the anomalies removed, he is the perfect human. Am I correct?"

McKinnon frowned. "That would be a probability, but there are so many things about the genome we still don't understand."

"Yes. Yes." The President waved his hand in the air. "Let me finish. Suppose we have this virtual man and he likes us, okay?"

"Okay."

"He is not restricted by all the frailties of haphazard procreation like you, Miss Smith and me. Therefore, he should be able to use all of the faculties given to him through the genetic processes, without the abnormalities that usually occur in human procreation. Would I be safe in assuming he would have excellent memory capacity and superior cognitive function?"

"I—"

"That's why we need him. With his brain power he could reinvent the sciences. Mankind only uses about ten percent of our brainpower. This virtual man is most likely unhindered by our shortfalls."

Marin smiled. The greedy, pompous idiot was thinking of the program as some type of superman.

"Have we got the programmer yet?"

"No one knows who he or she is," she answered. "They went by a code name of Bezalel."

"No. No. This Krumm fellow. I know you and Himmel need help in retrieving the program. That's how this whole thing started. Get him on the line."

Shortly the screen was split. The President in his arrogant self-importance on the left and Krumm in his gentle, intimidated demeanor on the right.

"Mike," Gates started. "I may call you Mike?"

"Uh, I go by Michael, Mister President," he answered softly.

"I hereby commission you to help McKinnon and Sharon Smith here to retrieve this missing program."

"That's Marin Schmidt." Marin interrupted.

"That's what I said, isn't it? Anyway, Himmel Pharmaceutical has managed to create a working human model out of the information from the genome mapping project of early this century. You're the best we have." He flashed an overconfident grin. "And for God and Country you must get this thing for us."

"To what purpose, sir?" Krumm asked.

"To save it from exploitation and misuse, of course." The President seemed to think that was a satisfactory answer. "The government is not always the bad guy, Mike."

"Michael, sir. And what will the good old government do with the program once it has it?" The programmer continued. "Will it shut the thing down, perhaps store it in some archive until all of us who are becoming associated with it are dead? Or will you exploit it too for, let's say, military purposes?"

Gates' face became a mask of constrained anger. "I can see we have some philosophical differences, Mister Krumm, differences that would be better discussed in the privacy of someplace like Camp David."

"Perhaps." Michael's features remained unchanged.

"Unfortunately, my schedule will not allow such a debate."

"How convenient, sir." He looked at Marin and McKinnon. "What are your feelings on this?"

McKinnon spoke for them both. "This program must be in our hands. Private industry cannot be trusted with something so complex. I agree with the President."

"And you. Marin, is it?" Their eyes met across the electronic distance.

Marin felt her heart flutter in a giddy schoolgirl sort of way. There was a commonality between them already. He could tell by her expression that she did not agree with the bureaucrats. "My job is to find out who the original programmer is and to return the program, or accessibility of the program to Himmel. I'm afraid my opinion about the program itself carries very little weight."

"Nice dodge. You don't agree with them, do you?"

How could she lie to a face like that? "No."

Gates rubbed his chin. "Have you two met before?"

"No, sir," they replied in unison.

"Then what's your hang-up with this program?" He seemed to be looking more to Krumm than Marin but she answered.

"Just think for a moment, sir. Within the framework of this program is a model man constructed from model DNA. Everything about him, both his body and brain functions, is just like us. He might well be a conscious entity. He, despite his form of existence, is a human being."

"'I think. Therefore, I am.' That sort of thing?" the President mused.

"Maybe." Marin seemed pleased that he had actually given her some of his time. "I can't form an opinion without actually talking to him. Still, the same ethics should apply. This is the United States of America, isn't it?"

"Of course." Gates face returned to that of the national spokesman. "What are you driving at, Deputy?"

"I'm a lieutenant, sir."

"Whatever. What is your point?"

"I think she's saying that we should allow the program to make the choice." Michael interrupted. "If it's human enough, it has the capability to choose."

Gates sputtered and coughed while McKinnon cut his eyes at Marin.

"It's a computer program," the Bioethics agent answered for himself and his president. "An assembly of information working together as one unit. It's a model."

"And what are you assembled from, Douglas?" Marin could not help herself. "What is DNA?"

"A nucleic acid molecule."

"That does what?" Krumm continued the questioning.

"Why," McKinnon shrugged, "it-uh—"

"You know what it does." Marin pushed him further into the corner. "It encodes hereditary information. It tells your body how to produce certain enzymes and certain cells. It tells it how to grow amino acids into a complex structure now known as Agent Douglas McKinnon."

"It programs," Michael finished. "You are the result of that program. Himmel's virtual man should be no different."

Gates looked out of the monitor at Marin and McKinnon. His face was a mask of bemusement as he stared at them. "So," he finally said, "can we count on you to retrieve this program, Mike?"

Krumm looked away from the pickup for a long moment.

"Well?" the President spewed. "I'm a busy man, Mister Krumm."

"So am I, Mister President. So am I."

ELEVEN

THE HOT WIND FROM THE SKY limo's landing jets lifted the silvery bangs that hung stiffly over Kyle Pierce's forehead like a misplaced pigeon wing. Geoffrey Wallrich raised a hand in front of his eyes to protect them from the dust, his receding hairline unaffected by the downdraft. Their time was now up. It was Wednesday and the chairwoman of the board was touching down on American soil.

It had been a hell-bent seventy-two hours since she had announced her coming and the two men were still in their original position. Long hours on Wallrich and his team's part had yielded nothing short of quick tempers and splitting headaches. He rubbed his tight brow as the whine from the engines died and the singular hatch raised into the air. His temples still throbbed from the stress.

Pierce looked at him. "You haven't taken anything? How ironic."

"What do you mean?" the researcher spat.

"The chief of research and development for one of the world's largest pharmaceutical companies can't take something for a headache. That's what I mean."

"I haven't had time." He continued to growl. "I've been working, unlike a certain chief executive officer I know."

Pierce smiled his toothy, Indianesque smile. "Oh, I've been working too, Geoffrey." He tapped the side of his head.

"Been trying to think of a way you can weasel your butt out of this mess, no doubt."

"No doubt." He stepped forward. "Here she comes. Watch your mouth. No finger pointing."

Lynda Zwicknagl stepped onto the low sideboard of her limousine. Pierce studied her muscular legs, following them up to her slim waist past her slight breasts to the round, tanned German features. Short blonde hair styled in a practical part to the left framed her smoky blue-grey eyes. A smile crossed her lips bearing bright, perfect teeth.

"Wilkommen, freuline Zwicknagl!" The CEO waved.

"Veile danke, Herr Pierce. Guten tag, Herr Wallrich."

Wallrich took her hand and tried to smile. "I trust you had a good flight."

"Oh, of course," she sighed.

"This way." Pierce directed them both to the elevator door that would take them down to the comfortable surroundings of the Administrative Building.

"I love New Jersey in May," she offered as she took in the scenery from the rooftop. "Especially our campus."

"Yes, ma'am." Wallrich tried to be bouncy. "It is beautiful when you get the chance to contemplate it. I—"

Pierce looked at him and frowned. "Will you be staying long enough to dine with us tonight?" he asked cordially.

"No," she replied apologetically. "I have reservations in New Orleans for dinner, then it's back to Deutschland. My niece is graduating from the gymnasium tomorrow and I promised her I would be there."

They entered the elevator. "I hope you have good news for me."

Both men fell silent. Their eyes suddenly finding the elevator car's carpet extremely interesting.

"I thought so," Zwicknagl said. "What all have you done?"

Wallrich cleared his throat.

"Wait until we get to my office," Pierce warned him. "This

is far too sensitive for elevator conversation."

They were the only three people in the office area. Jackie had made sure there were plenty of refreshments before she left. No one else was admitted beyond the door to her office and she was given the rest of the day off.

Lynda Zwicknagl took Pierce's chair and let him and Wallrich fight over which of the guest chairs they would sit in. "Let's dispose of any formalities, gentlemen," she started as she leaned back in the comfortable chair and crossed her well-sculpted legs over the corner of the desk.

Wallrich compared her actions to a queen bee asserting her authority as she moved into the egg-laying chamber. Grab a worker by the mandibles and make him feel her power. "I'd prefer it that way," he answered, forcing Pierce to redden.

"Very good." She allowed a smile. "I prefer straight talk. That goes for you too, Kyle. You don't have to sell me on my company. I'm not the customer here. Understood?"

"Yes, ma'am." There would not be a whole lot out of him.

"Wonderful. Now, Doctor, tell me more about our situation."

Wallrich rubbed his hand across the top of his balding scalp and leaned forward. "As far as we know, we still have a virtual human program within our mainframe. Bezalel, our mercenary programmer, has managed to lock us out."

"Has there been any effort to contact him?"

"Of course. That was our first action. Apparently he doesn't wish to communicate to us. All the numbers we had on file have been voided. We've contacted Web management, but they can't help us trace any of his communications without a court order."

"Which we cannot get without revealing the nature of the experiment. Hence, the agencies of the United States government will find out we have acquired genetic maps and have done an experiment of a questionable ethical nature."

"We know they are keeping tabs on us." Pierce smiled. "But they have nothing."

"So no outside agency has been told about our dilemma?" She leaned forward, lacing her fingers together in a delicate motherly manner.

Wallrich looked at the CEO who looked at the floor.

"Kyle?" Lynda asked as she picked up on the exchange.

"The local sheriff and I are golfing partners," he started slowly as he gingerly picked his words. "When Geoffrey came to me with the problem, I casually asked Hutchinson if he could help. I vaguely explained the sensitivity of the project to him and he said he would send us his best person to investigate the matter."

"This investigator has been here already?"

"Yes."

"And he has been informed about the program?"

"She," Wallrich answered. "Uh, Marin Schmidt is her name."

"German descent," Zwicknagl coughed. "One point in her favor. Has she been of any help?"

"No. We haven't talked to her for the past day and a half. She said she would be contacting some of her sources in order to establish Bezalel's whereabouts. She knows only a minimal amount about computers."

"But you told her about the man?"

"I had very little choice." The R&D manager sounded almost as if he were beginning to plead for his life. "We've reached a dead end. We don't even know if the program is still intact."

"They can't get past the encryptions," Pierce added.

Lynda looked at them both. "We should have seen this coming." She leaned back again, thoughtfully tapping her lower lip with her right index finger. "There was no backup program created. We never considered that the model might work, did we?"

"We had hoped." Wallrich seemed to relax.

"Did it work? Did either of you see it?"

"I got a glimpse of him before he was awakened."

"Awakened? You mean activated."

"No. He wasn't like a robot or a computer. He looked like a real man."

"He would fit that definition from a virtual perspective." Pierce tried to sound like he knew exactly what was going on now.

"Meaning?"

"Well, Bezalel worked with the program exclusively for nearly two years." Geoffrey stood up and began to pace.

"And you let him? You didn't check on his progress?"

"Nancy Phin is the project leader. She did all the communicating. I received daily reports. She seemed to trust this programmer. I've seen the models he has built of the heart, the lungs, the liver, the eye. They're all very impressive, very realistic. We can still access them."

"What do you suppose this programmer's motive was for preventing us from gaining access to the very thing we have paid him to build for us?"

"It's my guess that the man became all too real to him. Those people live in such a limited world anyway. It's easy for them to fall in love with their projects and not want to let go of them."

"Did we tell him what the project was for?" She drummed her fingers on the arms of the chair. A cigarette would have done her good. However, the puritanical Americans had laws against such things.

"Of course. It was all explained during our negotiations."

"Let's stop and reassess, shall we." She joined Wallrich on her feet. "We have a program that you have only seen once. You did not see it in operation."

"No."

"But there is something within our mainframe that we cannot gain access to. We assume it is the man program."

"Correct."

"A program no one has seen running."

"No one but Bezalel."

"So Bezalel told your people. What if Bezalel was not able to build a man from the genetic information we provided? I mean, if you think about it, to build something as complex as a human being would require billions and billions of bytes of information. Billions alone just to assemble a molecule, to represent an atom."

The researcher shook his head. "He found a way around that. There is a common data base within the system for the basic atoms of the human body. The program is designed in such a way that it relies solely on that data. Each cell was assembled from that shared information base. It really saved us a lot of space and money."

"One piece of information shared by every part of the model. Ingenious."

"Yes, it was. That's why I don't doubt that we have a man within our system."

"A man we can't get."

"Right."

"Well," she started back to Pierce's desk and chair, "since we've paid good money for the genome maps and for the monstrous computer system, I think we should continue with the project."

"We should?" Wallrich and Pierce asked in surprised unison.

"We should. Only we should do it on German soil. Germany does not have the restrictions on genetic information like the United States. There, we will be able to build a new model without federal worries."

"But what about all we've accomplished here?" Wallrich sat back down.

"It will have to be written off as a bad experience. This next time we will make sure the model is built in a more open environment. One where the programmer will be seen and will report directly to the head of research and development."

Both men nodded in agreement.

"As for the present system," she sat back down too, "retrieve what you can and ship it to the home office."

"And what we cannot retrieve?"

"If there is a virtual man within the system, and I say that with a high degree of doubt, he will simply be destroyed."

"That would be like murder, wouldn't it?" Kyle Pierce leaned forward.

"Virtually," the chairwoman of the board laughed. "But there has to be a body before it can be called murder."

"That is an ethical debate for the philosophers and artists," Pierce smiled.

"Yes, it is." She reached into her pocket. "Before you both leave, I want to talk to this Nancy Phin."

"Why?"

"I'll need a head of research who has had close contact with this project." She stood up, leaning forward, arms supported by her splayed fingers. "And I want you both to tender your resignation letters and fax them to me by tomorrow."

Pierce saw it coming. Wallrich gave him that much credit. He did not jump with the same shock as the researcher.

"Miss Zwicknagl," the CEO started. "We've had too long of a relationship to end it like this. It's obvious that I'm not directly responsible for this bungled project. Research and development is an autonomous entity within this corporation. You know that."

"I do, Kyle." She smiled at him, black widow-like, calculating. "And I would allow you to keep your job if not for one mistake."

Pierce raised an eyebrow. "Mistake? Me? I did not contract with—"

"I'm not talking about that. If you had contacted me, instead of your golfing buddy, when this occurred, we would still have a working relationship."

"Well, I am sorry, Lynda," he chuckled. "But I didn't realize you were such a micro manager. I felt I was doing the right thing and you would not want to be bothered by this incident."

"Until I was called before Congress?" she growled. "Kyle, I trusted you with this operation. This is our corporate headquarters. It's in the United States, it is obligated to follow their laws."

"Then why did you want the experiment run over here?" Wallrich butted in. "If we'd done it in Germany, we wouldn't be having this conversation."

"If the board had wanted the headquarters in Germany we would have moved it back after we bought Hoescht-Celanese out. Logistically this is the best place for us. You're both changing the subject."

"We're both losing our jobs." Pierce allowed his temper to brush the surface of his cool exterior. "And rather unfairly."

Zwicknagl shrugged. "I've given my orders. Scrap the computer and resign. If I have to fire both of you, you'll find it to be much more difficult getting on anywhere else." She glanced at her watch. "Now get Nancy Phin up here. My time is limited."

Both men complied with her wishes and left her in the office alone.

Wallrich said nothing to Pierce as they left the building. He still had one ace remaining carefully tucked up his sleeve.

TWELVE

MARIN TOSSED HER OVERNIGHT BAG INTO the small chair in the corner of her bedroom and watched uncaringly as it bounced out of the seat in a sloppy roll onto the floor.

She let her body fall across the bed. The trip to Washington had been draining. The conference with the President was a disappointment, but she did feel like there had been something useful come out of it.

Michael Krumm seemed intriguing. She had never met someone like him before. She was not sure what it was yet. She was not sure if there had been anything there at all. She rubbed her forehead. It throbbed with the hint of an oncoming headache. Maybe she was just imagining things. What had she expected? A hard-boiled computer programmer who was as emotionless as his creations? Could that be it?

The phone in her office buzzed.

"Perfect timing." She sighed as she forced herself to stand. Her watch said it was nearly midnight. "Who in the world would be calling at this hour?"

The screen lit up with the drawn features of Geoffrey Wallrich. "Good," he said as he looked her over. "I didn't wake you. We have to talk, Miss Schmidt. May I come over to your apartment?"

"You may not," she replied without thinking. "What's so important it can't wait until morning?"

"Stupid question." He tried to growl. Was his speech slurred?

"Have you been drinking, Doctor?"

"Just something for my headache." He forced a smile. "I get fired tomorrow and I need your help."

"It seems to me you need a good night's sleep. Let tomorrow take care of itself."

"No! You don't understand. I've got a sheet of the Web numbers that we used when we were in contact with Bezalel. I can't have them traced without help from the judicial system. You're with the Sheriff's Department; you're an agent of the courts. We can find this son of a—" He stopped short of a rambling expletive at her hard frown. "Sorry. We can find him, I'm sure. Then Nancy will not get my job."

Marin rubbed her head. "I'm sorry. No judges are awake at this time. I can press for an appointment as soon as I get in in the morning. Nothing better."

"Oh yes, you can," he snapped. "You just don't care about me. You couldn't give a rat's, give a flip whether I remain with Himmel or not. It's only the crime you're after, isn't it? People mean nothing to you."

"Go to bed, Doctor," she snapped back and started to break the connection and block any more incoming calls from his number.

"But they're going to begin shutting the computer down tomorrow!" he screamed. "The program will be lost! Destroyed!"

Her finger paused above the enable button. "Destroyed?"

"Yes. She said we should destroy the program if we can't get to it."

"Nancy?"

"No. Swic-Zwicknagl. The chairman of the board. She was here today. She's firing me and Pierce. She wants to absorb our losses as lessons learned and move the program to Germany."

It was Marin's turn to curse. She held her breath until the

words passed through her mind. If the program was dumped, the President would have no prize. She didn't really care if he got it or not, but the thought of a being, virtual or not, being wiped out for the sake of good business bothered her.

Karyn's face blurred into her mind. The baby she was now carrying faced the same fate. Marin shook her head and tried to clear her sister from her mind. Was she willing to go farther to rescue a computer program that might be considered as living than she was to rescue a true human life?

Both seemed to be matters of convenience to her. She had the options of calling the night court to get an order and lose sleep and to call Karyn back and lose an independent lifestyle. They were decisions that were totally up to her. No one else had to make them. No one else could.

She rubbed her forehead. The program had to be rescued from annihilation. "I'll see what I can do," she told Wallrich. "Now try to rest until I get the order."

His face bent into a lopsided grin as he broke the connection.

Tears crept over the tired lids of her eyes as she dialed the judge's chambers. She knew the baby had to be saved too.

"Judge Poempius." The stoic voice clicked on as soon as the connection was made.

"Robert, it's Marin." She used his first name whenever they talked. It was not good protocol, but after spending time as a classmate and sometimes dating over the years it was hard to call him by his title.

"Marin?" His voice gained life as his clean shaven, Anglican face materialized on her screen. His dark blue eyes seemed almost black as he smiled at her. "You on the night shift now? I hadn't heard there were any problems."

"No." She wiped her eyes. "Just keeping late hours. I'm working on a case."

"As usual," he scoffed mildly. "When are we going to dinner again?"

"I don't know. This thing has me pretty tied up. Maybe when I get it resolved."

"And if I help you now it will be resolved much faster, correct?"

"I wasn't going to say that, but yes. I need an order to check some computer transmissions."

"Local?"

"No. The person I'm tracking used the Web. I've got a source with some account numbers."

"That's international, isn't it?"

"I'm sure it is, but I think any court order will give me access."

"Is your fax on?"

"Just a minute." She leaned over and flipped the switch. "Yes."

"Okay. I'll fax you a copy and send one to the Web over the net." He reached over beside his screen and did something with his unseen arm. Her machine buzzed to life. "Done. Anything else?"

"No." She stopped, hesitating to break the connection.

"I can read that face, Marin." His voice became softer, more caring. "What's wrong?"

"Besides not being able to get a decent night's sleep after chasing all over the east coast?"

"Yes. Besides that."

"It's Karyn."

"She's still in Ohio, isn't she?" He had heard many conversations about her.

"Yes, locked away and now pregnant."

"That's not good. They'll make her abort if—"

"I know. She wants me to adopt the child."

"What about the father?"

"A quick bathroom fling. Probably some kid. She didn't ask his name."

"Right." He looked away again as he called up something

on his free-standing pad. "I can't block the abortion across state lines since she's not in a Federal facility."

"No. That's not what I need."

"You want me to okay some papers? Can you handle a kid in your line of work?"

Tears came again. "I don't know. I just know it's my flesh and blood too. I owe it a chance at life, don't I?"

"According to the laws of the land you don't owe it or your sister anything."

"The laws of the land aren't flesh and blood, are they, Robert?"

"No." He looked at her apologetically. "Sorry. The cold judge came out. The laws are pretty cold and heartless. However, they do have their place."

"In a cold and heartless world."

"Bingo. What do you want me to do?"

"Let them know I'm willing to provide for the baby. It will be more impressive coming from you and there won't be a big investigation."

"Oh, there will be an investigation. Extra mouths are a burden. The state would prefer to abort. They'll have to absorb all her prenatal medical costs now."

"I'll take care of that," she said almost reflexively. "I'm an old maid anyway. My type always has plenty of money to burn."

He chuckled. "Why don't you take me out to dinner then? A judge's salary—"

"Is better than an investigator's." She managed a brief smile. They usually went Dutch when they did date.

"That will make the adoption easier." He finished his business. "I'll have it to them in the next ten days."

"Ten days?"

"Two. Anything for the great Detective Schmidt."

"Thanks, Robert."

"No problem. Hey, I heard he pleaded guilty."

"He did." She shivered. "It was really strange. I think he has something up his sleeve. I asked them to keep an extra close eye on him. Still—"

"Well, you watch your back."

"I always do." She looked up at the clock. "I've got to go. Thanks again."

"Anytime." He smiled his perfect lawyer smile and broke the connection.

Marin did the same and leaned back allowing her eyes to close. Exhaustion swept over her like a flash flood.

A hollow buzzing filled the air as she lifted the baby from its bassinet. It continued until the bright white room began to tremble and shake. Marin held the tiny body close to her own as she sought shelter in a doorframe. Around her the room disintegrated. White lace curtains falling from stained glass windows into a jumbled pile of white marble, plaster and computer chips. A man stepped out from behind the falling curtains, knife in hand. The baby cried.

"It's okay," she tried to coo as she backed out into the hallway away from the intruder. "Earthquakes don't happen here much. It will—" She pulled the white blanket away from the baby's face so she could make eye contact and nearly dropped him.

Instead of pink flesh, she found cold plastic staring at her through stainless steel eyes. It stuck out its tongue. "You can't find me! Na na. Na na na!"

She dropped the bundle and then fought to catch him before he hit the shattered nursery floor. When the small body made contact it faded away along with the tangled room.

A strong hand wrapped itself around her mouth and—

Cold steel against her throat.

Cold air filled her lungs as her own scream woke her.

The phone was buzzing for her attention.

She hugged herself as a cold sweat coated her body. The room seemed to spin as she tried to reorient herself, thankful it had all been a dream.

She tried to laugh, but it came out a strangled sob as the phone buzzed.

"Yes?" She fought the urge to whimper.

"Are you all right, Detective?" She did not recognize the voice.

"Who is this?"

"I'm sorry." The voice smoothed out as her memory made the connection. "It's Michael Krumm."

"Hi." She wiped the sweat from her face. "You woke me up."

"Oh." Silence followed his embarrassment. "Don't turn the picture on. I'm really sorry. It's nine o'clock and I thought—"

"Don't apologize." She tried to sound perky. "You couldn't have known. Nine o'clock? Are you in Somerville?"

"Yes." He hesitated for another long moment.

Marin glanced at her reflection in the dark screen. Her hair was jumbled and pressed to one side. Dried sputum had left a trail down to her chin, making a spot on her blouse. No. No visual on this call.

"I'm at your office. Sheriff Hutchinson gave me your number. When will you be in?"

"As soon as I can shower and change." She started to get up. "Oh, I almost forgot. We've got a problem."

"I know." He shrugged verbally. "That's why I'm here."

"No. Besides that problem. Wallrich called me late last night. They're shutting the computer down at Himmel."

"They're going to dump everything?" His words became short and anxious. She could almost picture him calculating what to do.

"Yes. At least that's what he said. He was drunk when he called."

"Does your desk have a modem?" He stopped himself. "Stupid question. Of course it does. I need the number for Himmel."

"It's in my directory. My password is 'VanGogh.'"

"After the artist?"

"Yeah. I used to paint some."

His reply was distant. "I like art. I'm going to try to sneak into their mainframe from here. See you when you get in."

"Can you do that? We don't have a court order."

"Hey," he chuckled. "We're working for Uncle Sam now. We can do anything we want. Besides, I don't know if their big computer is isolated or not. If it is, I won't get in."

She smiled. She liked him already and they had not really met.

As her head cleared, she remembered Wallrich and called him. There was no answer at his number. She then tried his office. The line buzzed as if it had been disconnected.

"Funny," she said to herself out loud as she undressed and prepared to get in the stream of steaming hot water. "You don't usually write a resignation letter and leave immediately."

Maybe he was still sleeping off the effects of the liquor. She climbed into the water and closed her eyes letting her thoughts cascade in free association. The dream reared its ugly head as a distant memory. Nonetheless, it left her feeling uneasy. What had it meant?

The thought of her sister's face staring at her from the phone screen, happy for once, forced her to dwell on what she had committed herself to. A baby living in her apartment, depending on her for its every need.

She shivered. That was even scarier than the dream had been.

THIRTEEN

WHEN SHE ARRIVED AT THE SHERIFF'S office she found Krumm tapping furiously away at her desk pad. He'd stop, shake his head and then enter something else. His concentration was fully dedicated to the information rolling up the small screen in front of him. She had to clear her throat twice before he slowed and turned around.

Michael blinked twice and tried to reorient himself. The woman standing behind him looked like the one he had talked to over the conference call with the President. He rubbed his eyes. It was always different seeing someone firsthand. He smiled. She was cute, forty-ish, but well kept. Her petite figure had none of the flab he would have expected from an investigator. Always on the run, eating poorly, keeping bad hours, riding a lot, very little exercise. He stopped himself as he stood up. He was stereotyping again.

Marin watched him rise from the chair. He towered over her. He was a good six feet tall, square shouldered, muscular. Not her typical preconception of a programmer. She extended her hand. He took it in his. His grip was firm and warm, almost hot.

"Michael Krumm," he offered first. "You must be Officer Schmidt. Pleased to finally meet you in person."

"The same here, but call me Marin, please. We'll be working together for a few days and formalities will get in the way." Besides, she wanted to hear him say her name.

"Marin," he smiled. His face was gentle. The word came out soft and songlike, as if spoken by a priest. "Call me Michael then."

"Michael." She nodded then let go of his hand. "Any luck?" Straight to business. Idle conversation would come later.

"I'm into Nancy Phin's computer." A tone of disappointment hung at the edge of his voice.

"That's good, isn't it?"

"Yes and no." He sat back down. "She is the project head, but she doesn't have access to Adam."

"Adam?"

"The virtual human program. I'm assuming that's what they've named him. Her files have many references to that name." He shrugged. "It may not be. But that's neither here nor there. She hasn't got anything that might be a code into the mainframe. Or at least I haven't found one yet."

"What about other computers in the office?"

"I'm doing a trace right now. There should be a map of some sort telling how the lab system is laid out."

Marin found the extra chair that sat in the corner of her small office and pulled it over to the desk. "Why would they make it that easy to get into? You've only been at this a couple of hours."

Michael smiled sheepishly. "Uh, it wasn't easy. Well, it wouldn't be easy for any run-of-the-mill hacker to get into. I'm privy to some standard overrides that most of the general public does not know about. Some of the software was written by me or one of the teams I've been on at one time or another."

"But you're, what? Only thirty-one or thirty-two. There's a lot of software out there."

"But very few basic programs run all the systems. They have to be designed that way, with underlying standard software packages, so they can interact with terminals anywhere. If they weren't, the Web would be dead. Each

117

computer would only be able to speak to another one with its same language base. ASCI used to be the basic language understood by the computers, no matter who manufactured them. Now it's KUINT. Krumm, Urgus, Ingersoll, Nelson and Thomas. We wrote it."

"Oh." She sat back needlessly impressed. "And I suppose when you wrote the program you hid some keys for your own use."

His face flushed. "I see why you're a detective, Marin."

"And I see why you're the leading programmer in the U.S.," she quipped awkwardly.

Silence fell between them as he worked and she watched. Numbers that meant nothing to her flashed and disappeared across the screen. Strange words, some she had seen before when she had mispunched her pad, programming stuff, followed the numbers. Krumm read them like a novel. Occasionally he would hum approval or click his tongue as a new sequence rose and fluttered by. This went on for another hour before it was interrupted by the loud banging at her door.

It was Sheriff Hutchinson. She let him in, trying hard to ignore the political smile. He always liked to make friends with Federal types. He cleared his throat. "This man comes charging into my office and I haven't been introduced yet. Highly irregular, Marin."

"Sorry, sir. I only just got here myself. Michael, Sheriff Hutchinson."

Krumm stood briefly, making it obvious that he did not wish to be pulled away from the screen at that moment. He extended a hand and took the sheriff's. Gave it a quick squeeze, then sat back down. "Pleased to meet you."

"I just wanted to let you know that you can consider our facilities here at your disposal. Officer Schmidt is one of our finest investigators and I hope she will be of great service to you in your efforts to solve this crime."

Michael stopped tapping in instructions. "Oh no, sir. It's

quite the opposite. I'm here to help her. I'm her humble servant, if you will."

Hutchinson raised his eyebrows in surprise. "Really? Rising quickly in the eyes of the national government then, are we, Marin?"

She managed a shrug. "It's not all that grand, sir."

"Well, nonetheless," he clapped Michael on the shoulder, "I'm always glad to help Uncle Sam."

"And Uncle Sam appreciates it, Sheriff," Krumm responded. Marin could feel the sarcasm oozing from him.

Of course Hutchinson did not pick up on it. "Good," he smiled and moved back toward the door. "Carry on."

"We will," Marin smiled and folded her hands behind her back.

"Politician," Michael cursed under his breath as he continued to run through Himmel's systems. "Is he always that obnoxious?"

"Only when he's intimidated." She sighed. "He's actually a good administrator. We don't want for much here."

"He knows who and how to brownnose them." A few more key taps and a list she recognized began to flash up on her screen. "I believe I've found my way in."

She leaned down next to him. A musky scent filled her nose. Aftershave. A sweet smell followed that of the cologne and mixed with the fresh scent of soap. The smell of a clean man. She avoided the temptation to close her eyes. "I've seen these files before," she whispered.

Michael felt her warm breath against his neck. He closed his eyes. She smelled of light perfume and clean water. "What, uh, when?" he managed.

"At Himmel. They had the model of the heart on one of their desktops. It looked so real."

"Let's see if I can call it up."

His deft hands worked their magic on the distant computer and shortly a pumping heart materialized. Only this time it was much smaller because of the size of her screen. "Amazing," he whispered as he turned to face her. Their noses were mere inches apart.

Marin quickly stood up and caught her breath. "That's what I thought. And to think they've built an entire man."

Michael looked at her for a moment. His heart was beating a little faster than usual and it wasn't because of his discovery of the computer model. She was a compelling lady. Very compelling.

"Shouldn't we call McKinnon?" she asked, breaking the moment's fixation.

"Yes." He turned back around. "I should be able to get to the whole program in another half-hour or so. I'll need a number to download to."

"I'll use the next office." She turned and marched out. He watched longer than was necessary as she glided through the door, each step performed out of a feeling of comfortable familiarity. This was her world.

"Ask her out, you dolt," he commanded himself before turning back to the computer. "Nah! She'd never go."

A few minutes later she came back into her office and handed him a cryptic string of numbers. "This is what he gave me. I hope you understand it."

"Sure. It's the access number for the computer facility at Palo Alto. It's the only one big enough to hold all these megs. I'm going to have to try to set up a dual line via your terminal and transfer the information directly across country." He bit his lip. "I don't know if it will work with your system."

"Too small?"

"Way too small. The office doesn't own anything bigger, does it?"

Marin bit her lip. "No. We have to use the FBI unit in Newark if something big ever comes up."

He thought for a minute. His hands worked through his straight, strawberry blonde hair.

Marin felt tempted to rub his shoulders as he thought, but she did not give in. She was not going to come across to him as being too forward. He probably thought of her a mere cop anyway. Why add to that conception?

He snapped his fingers. "Okay."

"Okay what?" she asked reflexively.

"We can use this unit as a relay without a storage backlog."

"Okay."

"If I can talk Himmel's computer into compressing the data."

"Wouldn't they have already done that?"

Krumm shrugged his shoulders. "I don't think so. The numbers I'm getting point to a loose organization of the contributing software. They haven't taken time to manage the system yet. That's what happens a lot of the time when you first throw a program together. You want to get everything you can think of into the system, then once it begins performing, you worry about organizing it into something marketable."

"They hadn't gotten that far."

"Apparently not. Let's see what she'll tell me." His hands began to fly over the keyboard again as he gave the distant computer orders to compress the data it held.

Several long minutes passed before he backed away from his work. Marin had no idea what he had done but the screen now read "waiting."

"What does that mean?"

"It's following orders. The whole system is being reduced exponentially." He rubbed his head again. "For something this size it will take several hours. Can you lock your office?"

Marin had to force herself to breathe as their eyes met. "Why?" she blurted out.

"I don't want anyone to touch your unit. Is there any place to go around here where a person can get a good meal?"

She felt like she had the word fool written all over her face. "Of course. Yes! I know of several good restaurants. Do you like ethnic?"

"I prefer Italian, or meat and potatoes."

"Great. I know just the place." She locked the door behind her as they entered the expanse of the sheriff's offices. "It's a little out of the way."

He smiled. "At least it's on terra firma."

She smiled back realizing what he was implying. Just a few hours ago he had been out of the planet's atmosphere and before that he had been to the moon. "I'll bet you're exhausted."

"Close." His smile was shy and infectious.

"How long did you say it would take for the computer to do its thing?"

"Three, maybe four hours."

"Then how about coming back to my apartment," she said as if it had been her intention all along. "I'm not such a bad cook. You can stretch out on the couch and relax while I whip up something."

"I don't want to impose, Lieutenant."

"You're not. And it's Marin."

"Well, thank you, Marin." They reached her parking space and he opened the door for her before walking around to her little car's passenger side. "Thank you."

She had to shake him once when she finally stopped in front of her home. "We're here."

He rubbed his eyes, embarrassed by the fact he had fallen asleep during the short drive.

She led him to the door and showed him the living room and the sofa where he continued his nap as she went to work in the kitchenette. She worked quickly and quietly, trying not to disturb her guest. A funny feeling caught her as she placed the strip steaks under the broiler. She could not stifle the giggle that rose in her throat.

"Smells good." Michael's voice interrupted from the living room. "What's so funny?"

She could not tell him what she had been thinking, not yet.

"Oh nothing. I'm just not used to playing house."

"You're not the marrying type, are you?" He got up and walked the short distance over to the counter that divided the two rooms.

"I didn't say that." She closed the oven door. "I'm just not used to playing the domestic."

He smiled. "Well, I am."

"Meaning?"

He coughed. "Not what you think. In the off time, when I'm not hacking away at some computer somewhere, I keep a residence in South Dakota. I'm a pretty mean cook. Can I help you with anything? I make an excellent salad."

She stepped back and swung her arm out, presenting him with the kitchen. "Help yourself."

When they returned to her office three hours later, both were wearing sheepish grins. His quickly vanished as he looked at the screen and the man sitting beside Marin's desk.

The screen was blank.

"There you are!" Geoffrey Wallrich shouted as he rose from the chair flourishing a handful of paper. "I have been to your apartment, to Himmel, to the Web office and finally here. You were supposed to call me back!"

"I did. You didn't answer." Marin frowned and moved between him and Michael. "How did you get in here?"

"The sheriff let me in. I went after the transmission logs." He smiled wildly. "And I think I found Bezalel!"

She looked at the crumpled stack of papers. "Let me see those."

FOURTEEN

MARIN TOOK THE LISTS AND STRAIGHTENED them out. Line after line of location codes ran from top to bottom in neat columns. At that moment it looked like the gibberish she had seen popping up on her screen as Michael worked. It would take hours of careful study to map out each location.

"Oh, don't pay any attention to that stuff!" Wallrich jerked the forms out of her hands. "It's all on the map on the last page. Locations of each transmission site. But the one most frequently used is this one." His bony finger slapped hard against a badly scribbled circle within the borders of the state of Ohio.

"Troy, Ohio?" Marin frowned and looked at the other sites. They ranged from California to New York, New Mexico to Wisconsin. None of them were within the right-wing protectorates. "There's nothing there. I know. My sister's in jail not seven miles from there."

"There doesn't have to be. He simply connected up with us via modem and wrote the program on our mainframe. He obviously traveled a lot."

"Are you sure?" Michael interrupted.

"I'm sorry." Wallrich turned his attention toward the programmer. "I didn't get your—"

He stopped. His eyes narrowed and he looked at Marin then back at him. "You're the Ulysses guy, aren't you?" Then to

Marin. "What's he doing here?"

He took a quick look at her desktop unit. Anger washed over him like a mad wind. He grabbed the Web data and made a dash for the door. "I know what you're doing, Officer Schmidt!" he yelled as he opened the distant doors of the sheriff's offices. "I trusted you!"

She put her hands on her hips. "I guess our cover is blown," she sighed.

"Doesn't matter anyway." Michael touched the surface of the keypad. "We've probably lost everything. I believe they shut the system down in the middle of my compression sequence."

He tapped the "on" key and the screen flickered to life.

Marin saw the look of embarrassment that grabbed him and tried hard not to smile.

"Well," he rubbed the back of his head, "I guess someone just shut the screen off."

"I did," Sheriff Hutchinson said as he poked his head into the office. "I didn't figure you wanted Wallrich to see what you were doing."

"Why'd you even let him into my office?" Marin asked her boss, trying not to sound as angry as she felt.

"I didn't want to arouse any suspicions. He said he had some vital information for your case. I didn't think you two would be gone long."

Michael was already back at the keypad, lost in the world of Himmel's mainframe. "Thanks, Sheriff," he managed without turning away from his work. "Good thinking. Now, all we have to do is transmit this stuff before Wallrich runs back, squeals on us and they really do shut the system down."

Hutchinson winked at his officer. "Glad to be of service."

"Thank you, sir," she managed in a humbled tone.

"Just catch this guy. Kyle Pierce is a good friend, after all."

"Yes, sir."

Michael worked for another fifteen minutes before shutting

the computer off. "Okay," he smiled. "Now all we have to do is go to California and see if we can resurrect this virtual man."

"California?" Marin found herself taken totally off-guard.

"Yes," Michael smiled. "That is where I left Palo Alto. At least I think I did."

"But," she stammered. "I really need to look into the Web information. See if I can track down this Bezalel."

"That can wait."

"He's a thief, Michael. I'm a law enforcement officer. It's my job."

"And there's only one planet he can be on. Come on, we'll use the system at Rocketdyne to track him. It's bigger and faster."

"Well, I don't think Doug McKinnon drafted me to—"

"You're a Federal agent." He stopped her. "You can go anywhere the job requires you and now it requires that you go to Palo Alto."

She ran her hands through her hair. *Come on, Marin*, she told herself, *be a big girl.*

"Besides." Michael interrupted her. "I have an apartment out there and I owe you lunch."

She felt her face grow warm. Her eyes narrowed. "That's the real reason, isn't it?"

His smile was cavalier, strange for his face but fitting for the moment. "Yes, it is. Come on. I think you need a break. I know I do."

"I'll have to pack a few things first."

The flight west was an interesting experience for her. Since he was a National Aeronautics and Space Administration contractor he had access to the transportation facilities at Washington's Dulles Airport which was one of the few places that flew the new laser combustion craft.

The ship looked little like the passenger planes she was used to. Its long, flat body seemed to be made wholly of glass and plastic. Very little of the surface area was dedicated to the vane

126

needs of a typical airliner. The only window in the plane was on the door, which was also the only exposed metal. Two huge ramjets lined the belly of the beast like rectangular funnels.

Michael took her hand on impulse as they neared the hatch. "It's actually quite safe." He smiled as he showed his boarding pass to the crewman standing guard.

"But we'll be locked inside it. No windows." She shivered. "What if something goes wrong?"

"What if something goes wrong in a ship with windows?"

"I see your point. How did you say the plane worked again?"

He stopped at the edge of the bottom stair and pointed straight up. "Somewhere, about there," his finger stopped a few degrees east, "is a satellite that holds a powerful laser. When the captain of the plane transmits a signal to the satellite it will fire the laser at the plane. The surface of the ship is nothing more than a big lens which refocuses the energy from the laser beam into the combustion chambers back there." He pointed to two identical bulges at the back of the rectangular tubes. "The air inside the chambers is superheated and directed aft. This action forces more air in through the intakes and provides propulsion."

"And if the pilot loses the beam?"

He patted the glassy bulkhead. "Momentum will power the jets for a time, but this is a lifting body. The pilot and the computer will simply glide us in to the nearest airport."

"Have there ever been any accidents? Any planes burn up?"

"No the beam from the laser is diffused enough that it will not cause anything like that. In fact, we're probably standing in some laser light right now."

Marin stopped herself from looking up and hurried into the plane. "Okay, I'll trust it this time, but if something happens," she smiled, "and if we die…"

"You'll never ride one of these again. I guarantee it," he finished for her.

The flight was strangely disorienting. There was the slight sensation of pressure at takeoff and then silence. It was almost as if they were not moving at all. Marin found the fact that she could not see out to be very discomforting and tried hard to offset her uneasiness by sleeping.

That didn't work either. The craft was just too quiet.

"It bothered me the first time I flew on one of these too," Michael tried to reassure her. "You get used to it after about your third or fourth flight."

"You've been on one of these a lot then?" She eyed him through half-closed eyelids.

He shrugged modestly. "When you work under someone like Alton Treon you see things most ordinary citizens aren't privileged to see."

"Treon? He's the electricity guy. What did he invent, a new kind of wire?"

"A superconducting material."

"Superconducting?" She moved her seat back to the upright position.

"Yes. That means it is a material that provides little or no resistance to electrons as they move along it. It makes electricity easier and cheaper to transmit. With a superconducting coil, like Ulysses is using to make its way to the fringes of the solar system, the coil only has to be charged once and monitored with very little additional voltage in order to maintain the magnetic field the charge produces."

She frowned. "I'll take your word for it."

He smiled. "Oh, it's not all that hard to understand if you don't get into Tesla's theorems and all the other technobabble."

"What about you?"

"Pardon?" It was his turn to frown.

"I'm a people person, Michael. I don't pretend to understand half of the wonderful technology that makes our world hum. My life is spent studying, following, second guessing people."

"And what have you guessed about me?"

She raised her eyebrows. "I really haven't taken a whole lot of time trying. I do know, however, that you're a man of strong convictions. I saw that during our conversation at the White House. You're soft spoken until you get to know someone. You handle yourself in an almost priestly manner. You're probably Catholic, if not Lutheran. Your father is probably involved in the church in some way. You love life, especially your field. There are times it consumes you to the point where you lose contact with reality. You suffer from mood swings, but you manage to hide them from the few people who are around you. Shall I continue?"

Krumm looked deeply into her eyes. "Amazing. I'll start calling you Sherlock from here on out."

"No. Don't insult me. It's not you."

"Insult you? Why Sherlock Holmes was one of the greatest detective minds in literature."

"That's the point. He was a literary figure. Arthur Conan Doyle already had the crime figured out before he even began laying the clues down for his super-sleuth to deduce. Real life isn't like that. You get a peek here, a glimpse there. Maybe a witness. Most of the time you don't. Take my last case for example. If that vagrant hadn't seen the killer tap his last victim with his umbrella tip we wouldn't have him behind bars now. It was lucky coincidence."

"And it was good guess work that told you all that about me?"

"No." She gave him a sheepish grin. "I used my new clearance to read up on you after we talked at the White House."

"Why?" He leaned back in his seat. There was not anything in those files he did not know about. He edited them several times. "You didn't trust what you saw?"

"Oh no!" She turned to look out the nonexistent window at her side. "I—" She paused and bit her lip. No. She would not tell him.

"You what?" He put a hand on her shoulder and gently forced her to face him.

Her eyes found a spot just below his elbow. "I found you to be very intriguing."

"Intriguing." He said the word as if he had a piece of stale cracker in his mouth. "Intriguing."

"Yes. When we were talking to the President there was one moment when there seemed to be some kind of connection there. I don't know. It was like we saw the situation from the same point of view. The Adam program is a human life and all human life is precious and should be preserved."

"I do feel that way." He let go of her.

Silence fell between them. It lasted for nearly a half-hour as they turned their own thoughts over in their minds. Michael could no longer hide his attraction for her. He wanted to attempt to begin the foundations of a relationship, but wasn't quite sure how to establish such a thing. Marin, on the other hand, knew she could be open and honest with this man. His boyish innocence was merely a cover for a deep, caring soul buried behind the fascinating computer programmer.

"You know," she began in a low voice, "when I returned home after the trip to Washington I made a decision that will change the rest of my life. And it was all because of our conversation with the President."

Michael steepled his hands together in front of him and listened. "What sort of change."

"I'm adopting a child. It's my sister's."

His eyes brightened. "That's wonderful. Was she going to abort it?"

"The state was." Marin looked at the ceiling. "She's in prison and they automatically order an abortion for any inmate who gets pregnant during their term."

"I've never agreed with that." He chuckled. "Of course I've never figured out how a woman can get pregnant in a women's prison."

"Where there's a libido there's a way. She doesn't even know the father's name."

He took her hand. "That was tough for you, wasn't it?"

Marin felt her eyes warm with misty tears. "It hasn't fully sunk in yet. I guess the day I go after the baby it will hit me."

"When will that be?"

"I don't actually know. I haven't talked to Karyn since her call last week. I don't even know if she knows I'm going to do it yet. I had a judge draw up the papers for me."

"Hmm. Can you raise a child on your own? Statistics have proven that a fatherless child has little chance at becoming a healthy member of society."

"That's children born to teens who end up living off the Sharefare system. They lose educational opportunities and a chance to get their own lives started. That leads to a frustrated child and a life of social indecency. I'm educated. I have a good, well-paying job."

"A job that could one day find you dying of a gunshot wound."

"People die all the time." She found herself growing a little defensive. "My father drowned when I was five. Mother raised us with no problems."

His smile was genuine but critical. "You turned out all right, but what about your sister?"

"What about the thousands of criminals that come from stable environments? Mom and dad home all the time, a family dog."

"I don't think the numbers are that high."

"Well, what about my current case?"

"The mysterious Bezalel?"

"Yes. He seems to be a well-to-do computer programmer. What compels him to take a billion dollars worth of programming and destroy it? It's not his to take. I'm sure he was paid well for his skills. You of all people should know that."

Michael did not answer right away. Then he finally took in a deep breath through his teeth. "Do you know who Bezalel was? Do you ever read the Bible?'

"Sure." She frowned. "I don't remember that name though, but why should I? There are so many weird names in it."

"Bezalel was the only artist that I know of who was mentioned by name. He designed the Tabernacle and oversaw its construction, the same for the Ark of the Covenant and the High Priest's garments. He was a master at what he did and God and Moses recognized him for what he was."

"So this guy is a master at what he does and wants God and man to recognize him for that?"

"I don't know what drives him, but apparently his reverence for life has outweighed his loyalty to his contracts. We may never know what he came up with." He turned his head and looked toward the fore of the cabin.

She took his hand in hers. He was shaking. "Then again," she almost whispered, "we may one day know it all."

He pulled his hand free. "What is that supposed to mean?"

"I think you really understand this guy. I sort of do. I'm not very good, but I know what it's like to create something and then have to watch it go."

"You're an artist?"

"I used to paint a lot." She smiled. "You're an artist too, Michael. How do you feel about Ulysses leaving the solar system? You spent years of your life designing that thing. Now, for all sense and purposes, it is gone. You'll never see it again."

His eyes met hers. "It's almost like watching your child die."

"Exactly." She leaned forward and kissed him on the cheek.

FIFTEEN

WHEN THEY ARRIVED AT THE LONG, flat red brick computer center at Palo Alto, Michael was surprised to find security personnel circling the facility. Secret Service agents dotted the long walkway in from the parking lot, hiding here and there in the ornamental shrubbery. He had to show his ID ten times before he reached the lobby.

Marin had done the same. "Is it always like this?" she asked as they moved toward a set of steel doors.

"No. Not even when we were doing the initial tests on Ulysses' brain."

She slowed as she saw a familiar figure moving toward them at the other end of the white corridor. "I think we'll have an answer soon enough."

"McKinnon," Michael groaned.

"And he's smiling."

"There you are!" The agent's voice seemed too jovial. "We have been waiting for you for two hours."

"We?" Marin asked. "What's going on here, Doug?"

McKinnon gave him an overzealous smile and winked. "I called the President as soon as we, excuse me, as soon as Michael had extricated the program from Himmel and transmitted it here. I told him we had the artificial man and he was very excited. In fact, he dropped everything from his schedule today so he could meet Adam."

Michael felt his heart rumble in his chest. The flutter was the familiar arrhythmia he often felt when under stress. He tried to pay it little mind, but found it hard to ignore. "The President is here? In this building?"

"Yes. Waiting to meet the program. He's taking your suggestion and is going to personally ask him if he will work for the United States government."

"But I haven't even accessed the program yet." Krumm rubbed his brow. "You guys always jump the gun. All I simply did was download everything that was in Himmel's computer at Somerville. I don't know if I can find Adam or not."

McKinnon's face turned ashen. "But, I thought—"

"You jumped to conclusions."

Marin grinned and rolled her eyes as McKinnon's pleading gaze passed by her.

Then the agent's expression changed to one of resolve. He reached out and clapped Michael on the shoulder. "Well, I know you can do it. In fact, you will do it or you will never work again."

"Oh don't be so petty, Douglas," Marin growled. "You guys don't mean anything to Michael. He's helping you, remember? And so am I, for that matter. So, back off the machismo, super-agent bit. If he can't pull up the program, it'll be your butt not his. You told the President we had it."

"Yes, but he said." He pointed at Krumm.

"Nothing. I'm the one who talked to you. He was still working." She touched Michael lightly on the back. "I'd suggest you get the President into a game of golf or something while we see what we can do."

McKinnon looked at her in disbelief.

"That's the way it is, Douglas," she reiterated. "Now scoot."

The agent backed away as they continued toward the computer room. Michael waved to some old associates as he found the familiar terminal access point and slipped his jacket off.

"Thanks," he said quietly as he pulled a pair of gloves and some goggles from a drawer behind the small desk in the dual walled cubicle's corner.

"For what?" She knew what.

"For calling McKinnon off. I don't like it when I lose my cool."

"I can't picture that happening."

"It does and usually with bureaucrats. He was being asinine. They think they can order anything they want out of you without consideration of the cost or time involved. It will be good to get this thing behind me."

"Oh. Well, you're welcome. I guess. Though I'm not really sure I want you out of the picture so soon."

He blushed. "No. I didn't mean it that way."

She smiled and patted him on the shoulder. "I understand."

He slipped the gloves on and pressed a teal button on the desktop.

"What are you doing?"

"I'm accessing the virtual keyboard. I won't be any good to anyone once I begin working."

"Is there a lounge or anywhere I can wait?"

"I think there's one in the basement. You've got clearance. Explore the building. Have fun."

"Right. I think I'll find the President and see McKinnon dance."

Michael chuckled. "I wish I could go with you."

"Just find that program."

He shrugged. "It really shouldn't be that hard now. I just wanted to see Doug squirm." He slid the goggles down over his eyes and began moving his hands over the keyboard the computer was projecting in front of him in cyberspace.

Marin stayed where she was for a few minutes until the little ritual became too strange for her to follow. It did not take long to find President Gates. He was sitting in the middle of the facility's large control room, his brow and hands knit together in disgust.

"I assure you," McKinnon was pleading, "he'll have it soon. He's the best we have."

"Not if the original programmer was better. Do you know I had a call from Germany's chancellor this morning? Someone at Himmel told him we had stolen the program. The country is threatening sanctions if we do not return it."

"But they were going to destroy the program anyway."

"That's not the point." Gates stood up. His clean-cut demeanor seemed wrinkled. A few hairs were out of place. His jacket rode up on his hip. Marin wondered if he was having second thoughts about what he had done.

"The point is," he continued, "we have something that could be used for the furtherance of mankind or its ultimate destruction. We must control it. If Germany got a hold of it—"

"The rise of the Fifth Reich?" Marin offered.

Gates snapped his fingers and pointed at her. "You know she could be right." Then he frowned. "Do I know you, miss?"

"We talked by phone one time, sir. I'm Marin Schmidt. A special investigator on this case. Douglas McKinnon brought me in."

"Oh yes." He brushed his hair back with his fingers. "Now I remember. You're of the opinion this program should be treated as really human. Schmidt. That's a German name, isn't it?"

"About as much as Gates is, I guess." She remained in place so as not to spook the Secret Service agents closing in around her. "Why is everyone always afraid of Germany?"

The President shook his head. "A powerful people. Do you realize almost every advance in mechanical technology has come from the Germans? They've brought the world to arms three times in three centuries. They've always been conquerors."

"So we're all hopelessly paranoid when it comes to Germans." She crossed her arms slowly. "What about the Japanese or the Chinese. The Chinese especially. As far as we know they have their finger on the button to nuclear midnight."

Gates waved the comment off. "Neither is the economic giant Germany is. Overpopulation is their downfall. Since we've closed our borders to them, they're hurting worse and worse."

"More reason to attempt to conquer the U.S."

"Now who's talking paranoid?"

"Oh, I'm not paranoid, Mister President. I don't lose sleep over whether or not there will be another world war or not. Those are problems I cannot control. You, on the other hand, have something to say about them."

"That's why we need this thing." He pointed to the large computer screen in front of him. "If we can employ this mind to think us through these problems in international relations and maybe even invent a way the United States can be the dominant world power again. Can you understand what I'm driving at?"

"If I did not." She smiled. She could not believe how forward she was being with him. "Would my opinion matter?"

"No it wouldn't."

"That's what I thought."

"I like you," Gates said as he moved toward her. "How would you like to try out for a position on my staff?"

She blushed. "I'm flattered, sir, but Washington isn't for me. I'm going to be adopting a child soon and I don't think D.C. would provide the proper environment for its upbringing."

"Oh, the Governmental Citadel is quite safe. The rest of the city has little or no access to it."

"I know, but no thank you."

He shrugged. "Who do you work for again?"

"The sheriff of Somerset County New Jersey."

"And how did you get involved with this project?"

"Quite by accident. Himmel's CEO and Sheriff Hutchinson are friends. The crime was mentioned during a golf outing and the rest is history. Now I'm out here in California waiting to see if Michael can decipher the program."

He rubbed his chin. "Michael? Oh yes, Krumm. That's a German name too, isn't it?"

She shrugged. "We're both working for you, sir."

"Yes, you are," he smiled. "How's he doing?"

"I'm not sure. I just left him a few minutes ago. He was hooking into the system then."

"He did a bang-up job on the Ulysses project. Made the nation proud."

"I'm sure he did."

"Made Alton Treon happy too. Now, he wants permission to start on that froody colony ship project of his."

"Colony ship?"

"Yes. He wants to send man to the stars, himself included. He might as well. He's got the money." Another shrug. "And he is offering to give our space program credit for the feat. What do you think, Miss Schmidt? Should we sponsor a billionaire in a mad effort like that?"

"What does the nation have to lose?"

"We could get a bad reputation for mad spending. That won't go well with the world banks."

"How is the nation's reputation now?"

He looked at the floor. "Bad."

"Then we don't have anything to lose, do we?" She smiled. Was everyone in government this way?

"You've got the hang of it, Schmidt," Gates laughed. "You're telling me what I want to hear."

She found that to be insulting. "Not intentionally, sir."

"Sure you wouldn't consider a place on my staff?"

"Certain of it, sir."

"You're strong willed. I like that."

"In a woman?"

He raised a finger. "Ah ah ah. Don't try to catch me in that little gender-preference web. I'm far too experienced for that."

Marin managed a wry smile. She was not up to battling wits

with the President. Her eyes cruised down to her wristwatch. How long had Michael been at it? Surely not that long. Her stomach grumbled. It was nearly dinnertime back in New Jersey.

"I know," Gates said as he watched her. "I expected the thing to be up and running as soon as I walked through the door."

"No." She checked her wallet for her credit card. "It's not that, sir. If you'll excuse me. I'm going to find the commissary."

Douglas McKinnon coughed. She had not noticed him during her fencing match with Gates, but apparently he had been standing there silent and humiliated somewhere in the background.

"You know where it is, Doug?" She caught his hint. "Could you show me?"

"I'd be happy to!" he replied a bit overzealously. "This way."

They entered a corridor just off the main control room and went down a flight of stairs until they reached the basement level.

"A bit antsy, isn't he?" Marin referred to the President as they entered the small dining area. A counter featuring cold cuts plus a burger and pizza bar lined the wall on the right. Its human attendant rested wearily on a lone stool.

"That's an understatement." He pointed at a layered sandwich of beef and lettuce. "I thought he was going to choke me to death himself. Man, I looked like a fool."

She watched him greedily open the plastic covering and begin eating before she had a chance to order. It was almost disgusting. The man was definitely under too much pressure. Now more than ever.

The attendant took her order and promised the hot sandwich would be delivered to their table in a few minutes. She grabbed a drink from the dispenser and sat down. McKinnon dropped his trash in a plastic box on the way to their table and gulped down a steaming cup of something that didn't quite smell like coffee.

"Boy, you and Krumm sure hit it off right away." Douglas surprised her by changing the subject.

"Yeah." She took a sip of her soft drink. "He's not an egghead like I thought he would be. He's really a nice guy. There's a personality there that I get along with."

"More than that, I suspect."

She nearly choked. "Excuse me?"

"I saw the way you were walking close to him as you entered the building. I'm not unfamiliar with romance. After all, I am in the bioethics field."

"Which has nothing to do with romance." She grinned at him as the waiter brought her meal.

He sat silently looking at the nondescript pattern that lined the walls of the restaurant while she ate. She was slow and meticulous by his standards, but she probably did not have the ulcers he had. He needed to slow down. Maybe once the President fired him, his thoughts tortured him.

The small phone on his hip buzzed. "McKinnon," he said without removing the unit.

"You and Schmidt had better get back to the control room or you're going to miss it," one of the other bioethics agents warned him. "Krumm has come down from his office."

They piled their trash into the closest receptacle and ran back.

Michael sat poised at a real keypad. He looked up at Marin and winked.

"Okay, Mister President. This is what I found in Himmel's data."

The big screen that filled the wall above their heads buzzed to life. Slowly the image of soft tissue connecting to form pathways of greyish matter grew until it finally formed something resembling a brain. Next bone formed like growing concrete around the nerves, then muscle, eyes, tendons. A human was being constructed before them. Gates sat back and rubbed his chin. Others in the room gasped. McKinnon hugged himself.

When the man was finally completed, he looked down into the room and smiled. "Hello," he said in a voice that was radio announcer perfect.

"Greetings," the President said as he rose from his chair. "I am—"

The projection ignored him. "I am Adam. A.D.A.M. A program designed to allow you to explore the anatomy of the human body. You can peal away my skin at any point. Examine the cells within. Even see examples of human procreation, if you are over eighteen and your parents have entered the special code."

The President frowned and looked at Krumm.

"It's what I found, sir," he laughed.

"Now," the projection continued, "let us start with something simple like saliva. It isn't just water, you know. It is produced by special glands just below—"

"Shut it off!" Gates screamed. "Shut it off!"

SIXTEEN

GATES CLOSED THE DOOR TO THE small office with a violent shove. Marin backed away from him more out of reflex than fear. Douglas McKinnon tried hard not to make it look as if he were using her as a shield, but he strategically remained behind her in relation to the President. Michael sat comfortably in the lone chair behind the office's only desk, grinning.

"It's not funny, Krumm." Gates pointed his finger accusingly. "I have been made to look like a fool in front of one of the most elite staffs of scientists in the country."

Michael chuckled. "But it was classic, sir. You have to let yourself see the moment. We worked feverishly to rescue possibly the most complex program ever written. We hurl it into the nation's biggest computer, call it back up—"

"And get a child's anatomy program!" the President fumed. "This guy has made me look like a blooming idiot and I want him."

Marin could not resist, maybe it was Michael's attitude toward the whole thing, she didn't know. "How do you know it wasn't a woman's program?"

Gates glared at her. "Don't push me, Schmidt."

She swallowed hard and lowered her head just a bit. The President could be scary, even when not taken seriously.

"McKinnon, you got me into this," the chief executive paced around to the agent, "and it will be your job to get me out of this. I want this Bezalel drawn and quartered. Whatever charge you can come up with, whatever agency you need to help you track him down, you use it!"

Michael wagged his head.

"What is it now, laughing boy?" The President slammed the palms of his hands down on the desktop. "You know you're really getting on my nerves with your holier-than-thou attitude."

"Only because I know what you're up against. If you do catch him, which I doubt, you probably won't find anything to pin him down with. It's a joke."

"And so am I. Is that what you're implying?"

"No, sir. You're just too paranoid." He pointed through the door. "Those guys know what it's like to run into dead ends like this. They have a history of it longer than you or your ancestor's history. They're scientists for cryin' out loud. Stone walls are made for climbing or analyzing. Not for blowing up."

"Who's blowing anything up? I just want Bezalel to pay."

"For your personal embarrassment. You'd lock a brilliant mind like that away just to save face?"

Gates did not meet his gaze or respond right away. Then, in a slower, more deliberate manner he said, "He is a criminal. He embezzled a multimillion dollar program. He should answer for that."

"What if he just saved a life?" Michael's voice was low and guttural. It frightened Marin to hear such coming from the man she had quickly grown so fond of.

"We're not going to get sidetracked by that issue again, Mister Krumm. It's a moot point."

"Is it? Then why not handle this through the FBI or another agency? Why go through the National Bioethics Advisory Commission? It's just a computer program."

"That-that deals with the human genome." McKinnon bravely interrupted. "You don't know what can be done with that information. It can be dangerous."

Michael turned away from the two bureaucrats and shoved his hands in his pockets. "That information is available to anyone who has access to the World Wide Web," he said softly. "You, gentlemen, are just playing games. This is an ethical issue. One that deals with a human life."

Gates crossed his arms and stamped his foot. "You talk as if you were Bezalel himself, Mister Krumm."

"If I was?" He spun around and stared the President directly in the eyes. "If I wrote that program? What would you do?" He held out his hands, wrists up. "Arrest me? Send me away to Fort Powell? Well, here I am, Mister President. Take me. Save face. Make me a martyr in order to keep you up in the public approval poles."

"Knock it off, Krumm!" Gates said, his nostrils flaring. "That would be too easy and you know it."

Marin coughed. "Not to mention how much worse it would make you look."

"Meaning?"

"To think you had the culprit working for you the whole time, trying to steal something for you that he had already stolen. He'd led you down one blind alley after another. You'd look more like a fool then than you do now."

"See!" He pointed to Krumm. "She thinks I look bad and she knows what's going on! I want Bezalel!"

Michael smiled and sat back down.

"McKinnon?" the President asked. "Why are you still standing here?"

"Um." Douglas rubbed the back of his neck. "I'm leaving, sir."

"You too, Officer Schmidt." Gates nodded. "I want a word alone with Mister Krumm before I release him."

Marin followed McKinnon out into the hallway. The Secret Service agents eyed them carefully as they stepped away from the door. Their stoic faces gave no indication whether they had heard anything through the closed door.

A few minutes later Michael made his exit still smiling.

"What did he say to you?" Marin asked as she instinctively took his arm.

"He wanted to make sure I was not Bezalel."

"What did you tell him?"

He shrugged. "I told him I was capable of doing everything he had done and that I might as well be."

"It wasn't good enough for him?"

"I'm walking down the hallway with you, aren't I?"

She managed a faint smile. "Show me that computer. Let's find this guy and get this behind us."

He led her down another flight of steps into a section below the basement. His ID card opened a green door marked for authorized personnel only. Inside the large, faintly lit room was one man who sat staring at a green console. A bank of flat readout screens lined the walls in front of him.

"Hey, Michael!" the thin man said after a few seconds of confusion. "Long time."

"Yes," Krumm replied before motioning to Marin to follow him.

"Hello!" the man chirped. "How do you do? Wow, Michael, she's quite a looker. I'll leave if—"

"Can it, Paul! I came here on business. This is Detective Marin Schmidt. She's with the Somerset County Sheriff's Department."

The younger man scratched his thick black mop of hair. "Is that northern or southern Cal?"

"It's in New Jersey." Michael let his exasperation show.

Marin offered her hand. As her eyes adjusted and Paul took her hand and shook it, she thought she saw something familiar in his face and slender build. "Pleased to meet you."

Michael saw the look on her face as she studied the other man. "Paul is my brother."

"Oh!" Marin laughed. "That explains it. Where'd he get the black hair?"

Paul shrugged. "It grows out of these little holes in the skin on my head. They're called follicles."

"Knock it off," Michael ordered. "Our mother. To answer your question more seriously. I'm sure you can see why they keep him locked away down here."

"Actually," the younger Krumm interrupted, "I'm a systems analyst and I'm monitoring Michael's latest monster."

"How's she doing?"

"Everything is functioning nominally. That pilot program you wrote has given her an extra boost. She'll reach Martian orbital space in another two months."

"That's six weeks in front of the projections." Michael seemed excited to hear this.

Marin stayed close to him. "I'll assume you two are talking about Ulysses."

"Oh, you should never assume," Paul chastised. "It makes an—"

"Paul!"

"Right." He saluted his brother.

"Can you switch off of the Ulysses telemetry long enough to give us a search of the web. We're trying to find a mercenary."

"Sure." He went back to his station and entered a few commands causing the information on all the screens to clear. "Who are you looking for?"

"A hacker named Bezalel."

Paul entered the code name and ordered the system to finger the suspect. Soon a list rolled up on the monitors in front of him.

Marin studied it. "That's the same list Wallrich had."

"Of course." Michael rested his hand on her shoulder. "He got it from the same place."

"Now let's get more specific."

"Who is his customer?" Paul asked.

"Himmel Pharmaceuticals Somerville, New Jersey."

"Okay." He watched the screens and whistled. "This guy got around. There are no less than five hundred contacts."

"Sources?"

"Um." He looked at the data and called up another screen. "Smart bugger. He's piggybacked his transmissions."

"Where is he?"

A map materialized in front of them as Paul told the system to extrapolate from the carrier wave signatures. "There." A red light flashed on and off somewhere in western Ohio.

"Troy," Michael sighed.

"Home?" Paul asked. "I don't know anyone back there who could—" He snapped his fingers. "Didn't Jason Culbertson just move back from, oh where was he?"

"Culbertson?" Michael frowned. "He couldn't program his way out of the bathroom."

"Oh no." Paul's eyes lit up. "He's been away. Somewhere in Europe. They say he's mastered a new technique. Now, what is it?"

"Can you get me his address?" Marin asked.

"No, Marin," Michael protested. "You don't want him. He's—"

"He's the only lead I've got right now. McKinnon will find out too."

"Neurosynotasking!" Paul burst out.

"What?" Michael turned to look at his brother's smiling face.

"That's what they are calling the new programming technique Culbertson has learned."

"Oh."

"It's supposed to be faster than the stuff you do, oh genius brother of mine."

"Nothing is faster than me."

"Don't be so sure."

"Come on," the elder Krumm told Marin. "Thanks, Paul."

"Oh, no problem. Nice meeting you, Marin."

"Nice meeting you, Paul."

Michael stepped through the door and back out into the narrow hallway. Douglas McKinnon stared at them as they turned toward the steps.

"Hold it!" he ordered.

They stopped. Marin turned to face him. "What, Douglas?"

"Give. Who is he?"

She looked at Michael. He shook his head. "Let us go to him first, Douglas," he finally said. "I'll need to look at his system."

"Why?"

"The Web has him tracked, but the Web can be wrong. I don't think it would be a good idea for you guys to go charging in on him unannounced. If he's the wrong person, your president will look even worse."

McKinnon did not like the idea. "No. You tell us now or I'll have you up on obstruction of justice charges."

"There ain't no justice," Krumm barked. "Come on, Marin."

She stood her ground for a moment. She could not find it in herself to be completely rebellious. "He's in Troy, Ohio. Tell your agents in that area to be ready. I'll call after we've confirmed it's him."

McKinnon shrugged. "That's better than nothing."

"Don't jump the gun, Douglas," she added. "Or we'll warn him and you'll have nothing."

McKinnon raised his hands. "I'll wait in Dayton for you."

The couple raced up the stairs and out to the parking lot. Marin could tell Michael was not at all pleased with what she had done.

"I had to tell him something," she said as they climbed into his car. "I'm still an officer of the law, regardless of my opinions. I'm bound to certain actions."

He pressed the charge release button and squealed out of the parking space. "And so am I, Marin."

"What is that supposed to mean?"

"It has something to do with a secret brotherhood of sorts.

148

An unspoken oath to stand by all those who share similar professions, dreams and goals. I want Culbertson to have a fair chance and I know how justice works in this country. If they want a scapegoat, they'll make him one. That won't be equitable. We have to get to him today."

"But we just got here. Can't you call him?"

Michael shook his head. "I have to see him personally. We made a deal."

SEVENTEEN

GEOFFREY WALLRICH LOOKED AT THE MAP in front of
him as his car sped north on Interstate Seventy-five. He had left
Dayton International only minutes before and was fast
approaching Tipp City. The map read ten miles to Troy.

He checked over the information he had downloaded from
the Web and looked at the portable map of Troy again.
Buildings blurred by him giving away to the occasional
sprawling flatness of corn fields and freshly turned black dirt.
Tipp City blossomed into a blast of skyscrapers then dwindled
into more corn fields. Ohio, at least this part of it, was flat and
uninteresting. In fact, he could not remember anywhere else he
had been that had seemed so tabular.

The fellow he was looking for went by the name of Jason
Culbertson. He checked the address against his portable map.
Market Street ran through the center of town. He found Water
Street and matched the point where they crossed. That was his
destination.

The car slowed on its own as it approached the off ramp that
would lead into Troy. He folded his papers and reached for the
small box he had tucked away between the layers of his
briefcase in the section normally reserved for his personal
computer. The box fell heavily into the seat and bounced onto
the floor. He found himself flinching.

He laughed to himself. "Idiot. It's not loaded."

The car came to a halt and warned him that the street system in Troy was not under the International Autodrive System. He released the cruise control and took the wheel in his sweating hands. There weren't many towns who had invested in the I.A.S. The system was only practical on long stretches of highway. He turned down the long road and casually entered the edge of the city.

From all appearances Troy was a town locked in its past. The constructs at the town's edge were left over from the economic boom of the latter decade of the previous century. As he got closer to Troy's center, he found buildings going back into the nineteenth century. He enjoyed the view as his car hummed into the town square which was surrounded by ancient buildings. To his left he could see the dome of a central government building, probably an old courthouse saved from destruction for some sentimental reason. He got caught in the inner loop of traffic which circumnavigated the non-functioning fountain, making three or four orbits before figuring out how to free himself enough to head north to the next block.

He was pleasantly surprised to see that he was on Market Street when he crossed Water Street. His eyes locked on the two-story nineteenth-century brick house on the eastern corner. There were no less than five dish antennas on the roof. He grinned as the car rose onto the bridge crossing the Great Miami River. He had his target and would soon be back in the good graces of his employer.

The plane touched down with a sudden jar. Marin looked over at Michael who had ignored the bad landing. He held his phone in his hand and dialed Culbertson's number while the pilot applied the jet's brakes.

Outside the small windows Marin could see the familiar shape of the Dayton International Airport terminal. How many times had she landed here with her mother on another of their long treks to visit Karyn? She had lost count.

"Nuts!" Michael said as he clipped the phone back into his pocket.

"Not home?"

"No. He didn't leave a message either. I'll try to get into his calendar once we get a room and I can access his home base."

The drone of the pilot's voice interrupted them as he thanked everyone, gave the local temperature and time and opened the hatches.

Michael was up before the woman finished her spiel, standing next to the opening doors. Marin did her best to fight the rising crowd and catch him. It was surprising to see this many people coming to Dayton. She could not remember that much that was still here to attract such an influx. The air show was not until June.

Michael was standing next to the security gate with an Avis cart at his heals. Their luggage was already on it. She knew better than to ask how he had accomplished this small miracle and jumped onto the little seat beside him.

"You really think Culbertson is in danger, don't you?"

He swung through an opening in a line of passengers, ignoring their shrieks and expletives. "I just don't want him to get stuck with something he didn't do. It wouldn't be right."

"You're certain he's not Bezalel."

"Yes."

"You still haven't told me what you meant about the deal you have with him."

"No." They swerved past the baggage pickup area and out into the rent-a-car garage. "And I don't intend to."

"A brotherhood of hackers," she grumbled as the small cart squealed to a stop.

"Your keys, Mister Krumm," the permanently smiling attendant said as he spewed two small cards out of his plastic mouth. "Have a good drive! Thank you for using Avis-Penske! We're here twenty-four hours a day, seven days—"

The robot's voice faded as they loaded their belongings into the back seat and chirped out of the garage. Traffic was heavy as they pulled onto the interstate. Michael checked his watch.

"Five fifteen." Marin sighed. "Good timing."

"Right." He made a hard left at the next exit ramp and headed back toward the airport.

"Where are we going?"

"The back way." He drove back into the small town of Vandalia and turned north as they reached the old highway Twenty-Five A. "We'll get to see a lot of country this way. You'll enjoy it."

"You forget. I've been here many times before."

"That's right. Your sister." He took time to look over at her and smile. "After we get this thing with Jason resolved, we'll run up and pay her a visit."

Marin grinned. *What a sweet man.* "That would be nice. Then I could tell her face to face what I'm going to do."

Michael's attention was now back on the road as it rose and dipped through depressions in the otherwise flatness of the Miami Valley floodplain. Outside the windows ancient farms and farmhouses flashed by telling them of a simpler time when the population was sparse and agriculture was king. In an instant the serene countryside gave way to blocks of industrial parks before being replaced again by fields of corn, wheat or soy beans.

"This was a good place to grow up," Michael mumbled as he took in the changing landscape. "But I wouldn't want to live here."

"Why not?" Marin wondered as they passed another two-story brick Victorian home. "It looks peaceful enough."

"Oh, I'm sure it still is, but you can never trust the economy here. There's so much invested and so much that can be written off. It's happened more than once."

"Is that why you left? You lost your job?"

He laughed; his gaze going somewhere beyond the road

they were traveling. "No. I was a prodigy. I didn't have to worry about the failings of local businesses. I was recruited by the nation's best."

"Then who?"

"Who?"

"Yeah. Who did you know that was affected by the economic climate here? You obviously don't like it because it hurt you in some way."

He flew through an intersection after the light had turned red. Horns blared at them as a large carrier nearly missed hitting Marin's side of the car.

"Hey!" she screamed. "Snap out of it, Michael!"

"Out of what?" he asked as they continued on across the countryside.

"You didn't see that light back there?"

"What light?"

She shook her head. "Michael. Come back to the present. It's twenty eighty-four.

"Let's stop and catch our breath. Your friend isn't home anyway."

He blinked and looked at her. His face was flushed with embarrassment. "I'm sorry. This happens every time I come back. I get lost in the way it used to be." He shrugged and pulled into a restaurant parking lot. "That's why I don't come back much."

She unbuckled her seat belt and opened the door. "Sounds like a good time to stop and eat."

He felt his stomach rumble as he looked up at the old Cassano's Restaurant sign as it flashed against the cobalt blue sky. "A sub or pizza would be good."

She closed the door and waited for him to exit the vehicle before walking over and taking him by the arm. "They've got one of these in Piqua," she said, commenting about the restaurant. "They've been around at least a hundred years. No other pizza like it."

OF ADAM

He smiled again. "Is this a date?"

"You want it to be?"

They walked in and took a table next to the window. The menu glowed from just over the large ovens behind the counter. Two attendants sat talking inaudibly as they waited for Michael or Marin to come up to them and order.

"I want one with all the junk on it," Marin said as she stared at the plastic letters. "And I'll have a Birch Beer."

"You're in the Midwest," he reminded her. "Sounds good, but you'll have to settle for Root Beer or something stronger."

"I don't drink alcohol," she whispered. "But a beer sure would taste good with those tall, greasy squares and that salty crust."

"Next best thing." He finally stood up and walked over to the counter. After placing his order he came back with a frosty pitcher of golden liquid. "It's nonalcoholic, but it's got the proper taste. I'm not much of a beer drinker either, but I do like the taste every now and again."

She took the glass he offered her and let him fill it. The drink was bitter at first but it did not take long for her palate to adjust to it. After the pizza came she decided to try and find out what it was that had driven Michael away from his home. She told herself it was not prying, just part of getting to know him better.

"Now, where were we before that semi almost ended my career?"

He blushed as he took a bite of the loaded crust. "I'm not following you."

"You left Ohio because of something that hurt you. Who got burned by the system?"

His face twisted into a mask of deeply buried pain. He took a deep swallow of his near beer and coughed. "Let's not be too delicate, huh, Marin?"

"I'm sorry." It was her turn to be embarrassed. "I-well, I just want to know more about you, Michael. I want to know what makes you tick."

He waved his hand. "No need to apologize. I just don't talk about it."

"If you don't want to now—"

"No. Maybe it'll do me some good."

She took another bite of pizza and another sip of her drink and leaned back in the seat.

He admired her brown eyes and her petite figure for a moment then took another swallow of his beverage. "My grandpa was an engineer with Bruckair Aerospace for twenty-five years. He was the one who moved the family to Ohio from Minnesota. Bruckair had given him plenty of work and paid him well."

"You and he were close?"

Michael shrugged. "Paul and I loved to listen to him talk about what he did. He would even take us to the plant where he worked and let us see some of the test data that he used. It was all very exciting for a little boy whose thoughts existed in cyberspace."

"So what happened?"

"Well, a year before his retirement, management decided to downsize. Even though he had seniority, they said he was too old to adjust to the new form of administration they were bringing in. They canned him. That made him ineligible for his retirement benefits." He took another drink. "He had given his life to that company. It was all he talked about. He used to brag about being a senior engineer with them. It was his life. And it was suddenly gone."

Marin looked into the bottom of her glass and watched the tiny bubbles float in a long stream to the surface of the brew. She had heard stories like his before. It had happened in her family. Her own father had suffered such a blow while working with New York Edison. But she remained near her home. It had not been enough to force her away. That sort of thing was a part of living, wasn't it?

"Anyway," Michael continued, "Grandma found him the

next week out in the garage. He was wrapped in the car's recharge cables. The coroner ruled it an accidental electrocution, but Grandpa was too smart to let himself get tangled up like that. He was only sixty-five. His reflexes were as good as mine."

"You think he killed himself?"

"You should have seen him when he came home after his last day at Bruckair. He was devastated. No one could talk to him. He didn't work on his computer anymore. When I visited him it was just like he looked straight through me. We had no common interest left, or so he must have thought. No. His death was not an accident."

She tentatively touched his hand. "I'm sorry."

"Yeah, me too. I guess that won't bring him back though."

"No." She took another drink. Her appetite had faded. "What happened to Bruckair?"

"They folded about five years later."

"Really? What caused that?"

"Some screwed-up accounts, missing funds. They arrested one of their corporate vice presidents after the company was declared insolvent." He finished his drink and looked at his watch. "We better get going."

She watched him for a moment. Too many years of interviewing suspects had taught her how to read a person's body language and his was screaming that he had not told her everything. She guessed he had had something to do with Bruckair's failure.

"What did you do with the transferred funds?" she asked casually as she stood up and followed him to the counter.

"They're still—" He stopped and spun around. His mouth split into a wide, toothy smile and he laughed. "You're good, Detective."

"I told you," she smiled back. "How did you do it?"

He slid his credit voucher into the pay slot and grabbed the receipt. As they neared the car he stopped again. "I didn't steal their money. It wasn't mine."

"I'm relieved to hear that. What happened to it?"

"Oh, it's still there in their accounts and on my grandpa's hundredth birthday it will mysteriously reappear for all the Bruckair heirs to fight over." He opened the door for her and made sure she was seated. "It was my gift to him. He didn't deserve to be screwed over like that. None of us do." The door clicked into place and Michael walked around to the driver's side and climbed in.

"No." He turned the motor on and slid the drive into gear. "And I know I do not deserve the right to be judge and jury. It was a rash act, one that only a teenager could be responsible for."

"You've thought about it then?"

"Of course." He merged them back into the light traffic of the rural highway. "And I've even had days when I would have gotten back into the bank's system and restored every credit to them."

"Why didn't you?"

He grinned and tapped his temple with his free hand. "I lost the encryption code."

"You didn't write it down?"

He shook his head. "I was a kid. I wasn't responsible for my actions."

"Yes, you were," she chastised. "You were a boy genius. You knew exactly what you were doing."

"Yeah," he conceded. "Just like I do now."

EIGHTEEN

GEOFFREY WALLRICH BACKED THE CAR INTO the vacant parking space and shut it off. He opened the probe box and got out, carefully attaching the cable to the recharger. He had found a spot a half block away from Culbertson's house where he could watch and wait for the man to either go in or come out if he did not answer the door.

His hands were shaking as he pulled the pistol out of its case and slipped it into his pants pocket. He had dressed casual so he would not raise suspicion. His jeans were loose enough to hide the bulge of the weapon when he stood back up. His heart pounded violently in his chest. He was not sure he wanted to do this. Was Himmel worth it? Was his pride?

He closed and locked the door.

A Miami County Sheriff's Department car whizzed to a stop beside his. Wallrich jumped as the officer rolled down his window and spoke. "You might want to move your car, fella," the mustachioed man suggested. "This is a bad corner."

Geoffrey forced a boardroom smile across his face. "I'll just be a few minutes, Officer."

"Okay." The light turned green. "It's your car. Have a good day."

"Thank you." He waved and moved toward the crossing.

From where he stood he could see only one entrance to Culbertson's building, but there was probably one other way out. Fire codes would demand it. He smiled, but of course there were no such codes when these buildings were erected. The light signaled for him to cross.

He could not ignore the scraping of the gun against his thigh. It was good he did not have to walk far. His leg was already irritated, though he could not say if it was specifically because of the pistol. He could feel the sweat clinging to the palms of his hands making them feel sticky and dirty.

He crossed Water Street and walked up to the entrance of the building. The door opened as he approached it. A young male receptionist greeted him as he poked his head through the frame.

"Can I help you?" he asked cordially.

"I-I'm looking for a Mister Jason Culbertson?"

The man leaned back in his chair. "He rents the upstairs apartment. The door's on the side of the building."

"Thank you." He backed out as quickly as he could.

"But I don't think he's home." The young man's voice followed as the door closed. "He usually goes out for his—"

Wallrich did not hear the last part. He made a B-line for the small stoop and old wooden door. There was no doorbell so he knocked as hard as he could. He heard the sound of a small dog barking from the top of the stairs but no one else replied.

"Excuse me." The receptionist poked his head around the corner of the building. "I don't think you heard me. Jason usually goes for a run about this time every day. He's not home."

"That's okay." Wallrich forced another smile and sat down on the cool cement stairs. "I'll just sit here and wait for him then."

"Whatever suits you, sir, but Jason is a marathon runner. He probably won't be back for hours."

"Oh." He started to rise and then realized the outline of the gun might become visible. "Well, I'll wait a few minutes anyway, then I'll be back."

"Suit yourself." The youngster waved. "If he comes in and you're gone should I tell him you were here?"

"No. I want it to be a surprise."

The receptionist frowned suspiciously.

"We used to work together. I was just passing through and wanted to surprise him," Wallrich lied. "Don't ruin it."

The young man's head disappeared and he was left to sit in silence. He stayed there for a quarter of an hour before finally getting up and stretching. He did not want to go very far from Culbertson's apartment, but he did not wish to stir up any more suspicion by sitting there for hours on end. He shoved his hands in his pockets and walked behind the building.

He had noticed a park of sorts there and decided it would be a pleasant distraction. He stopped to read the plaque before entering. "The Lois S. Davies History Park," it read.

It seemed Davies was well known in the late twentieth century for her oral history of the 1913 flood which devastated most of the Miami Valley. The rest of the placard told a bit of her life's story and why the land had been turned into a garden. He walked in and read the other displays that told of the history of both Davies' family and the region. It was no wonder the town looked like it was locked in time. Their heritage was almost as important as their well-being.

An hour later, and quite a bit more enlightened as to why Culbertson would base himself in such a burg, Wallrich found another seat facing the lazy green waters of the Great Miami River.

He immediately noticed a path that ran parallel to the river on the opposite side. There people ran and rode bicycles, walked and stood staring at the water. Like him, their thoughts were probably miles away. It was very relaxing. So relaxing, in fact, he almost forgot who he was waiting for and what he had planned to do.

Michael put the phone back in his pocket as they drove over the bridge. "That was his place back there, but he's not home. He's probably out running."

Marin looked out of her window at the passing quaintness of the small Ohio town. She thought she recognized the man sitting on the bench next to the river, but by the time they were over the crest of the bridge she had lost him.

"What is it?" Michael asked as he heard her gasp.

"I'm not sure. I saw someone I thought I knew."

"Here?"

"I know. Can we turn around?"

Michael turned into a long parking lot at the edge of a pair of soccer fields at the other end of the bridge. He swung the nose of the car around and darted back out into traffic. As they reached the southern end of the bridge again, he slowed so she could get a better look. The bench was empty.

"Go around the block. Maybe I'll see him again," she said as she anxiously craned her neck out the window, searching for the familiar face.

He turned east on Water Street and followed it up to the next block where he was forced to turn right. "The other way leads right to the river," he commented as they reached Main Street.

Then it was back around the square and north.

Nothing.

"Oh well," Marin sighed. "That'll bug me to death until I find out who that was."

"Maybe it was a ghost," Michael said sarcastically as they traveled over the bridge again. "This town is full of them."

"For you maybe," she quipped. "I don't know anyone here, remember?"

"Yes. I remember." He turned left on Staunton Road.

"Where to now?"

"Jason is a marathon runner. I'll guess he does the leg between here and Piqua as his workout. It's fourteen miles round trip. We'll drive out to Piqua-Troy Road and follow it in.

See if we see him."

"That's the road that goes by the Women's Center, doesn't it?"

"I think so. You want to see your sister tonight?"

"We'll be in the neighborhood."

"Okay."

The sun had started its long late spring trek down toward the horizon as they reached the great pit that housed the Women's Correctional Facility. It was well after visiting hours, but Marin knew her newly appointed federal authority would get them in.

The vice administrator insisted on seeing them herself before she allowed one of her former trustees to see a relative. Marin was impressed by the woman. Her name was Gwenevyre Harris.

She was a large woman who would easily fit the old cliché of a women's guard. Her thick black hands seemed like steel vices as they took hers in welcome. Yet her smile and voice were soft and genuine. "All the way from New Jersey?"

"In a roundabout way," Marin confessed. "We arrived here from California. We're currently working on an investigation."

"Karyn never told me you were a Federal agent," she said as she moved gracefully over to a small bar. "Coffee?"

"Thank you."

"You, sir?" she smiled at Michael.

"Uh, no thank you."

"She doesn't know I'm working with the Feds." Marin continued. "It's a recent commission. Hopefully temporary."

Harris sat back in her chair. Its springs protested loudly as she let her weight settle fully on the frame. "I see. How long will you be in the area?"

She looked at Michael. He shrugged. "It's all according whether we get our man or not."

"Oh! A manhunt."

"We're looking for a good guy," Michael said as he found a seat next to the window that overlooked the exercise yard.

"And our schedule is kind of tight."

"So you'd like to see Karyn now."

"If at all possible," Marin added. "It will be a surprise for her."

"As it is for us. You know she's pregnant, don't you?"

"Oh yes. She called me and told me herself."

"Asking for you to take charge of the baby when it's born, I assume." She shook her head as she reached for the intercom. "Section Twenty-two. Bring Karyn Schmidt to Visiting Area One."

"Acknowledged," came a tinny reply.

"You know where that is?"

"Yes, ma'am." Marin placed her cup of coffee back on the bar top. "I've visited her before."

"You know, Ms. Schmidt, if you knew what was good for your sister, you would not take the child."

Marin stopped. "Excuse me?"

"She's never going to learn responsibility as long as her family continues to rush to her rescue."

"I am not rushing to her—"

"It is our recommendation that you allow her to go through with the abortion. The mental anguish will teach her a valuable lesson in her sexual accountability."

Marin felt the blood rising in her cheeks as she let the cup drop the rest of the way to the counter. It swayed and then toppled, spilling the liquid onto the tile floor. "Sorry."

"Oh, that's okay. One of the girls will be in shortly to clean it up."

"No. Not that. I'm sorry you see things the way you do, Miss Harris. For your information I am not doing this for Karyn. I'm doing it for the baby."

Harris raised her eyebrows. "Really?"

"Yes, really. That child has more of a right to live out a full life than you have to condemn it. You're all alike, you short-sighted bureaucrats. You see things in numbers only. That baby does not deserve to be punished for its mother's indiscretion, or yours for that matter."

"Mine?"

"Yes. By any other name it's murder, Miss Harris."

The vice administrator screwed her face up into an ugly frown. "I've heard that argument before, Miss Schmidt. It seems to me it can be heard on those broadcast coming out of Utah and the other ultra right-wing states. It's your kind who murdered good doctors, coerced women to stay away from safe clinics. Abortion was the rallying cry of the Christian right for years. It still is, if you listen to their broadcasts.

"And those same holier-than-thou, self-righteous, so-called Christians would not lift a hand to help a poor, starving family, or even offer to adopt one of the children they fought so hard to preserve. How can someone like you find a job working for our fine government?"

"I am adopting one of those children, Miss Harris! So, don't categorize me into some group you know little or nothing about. I am a Christian and I was picked as a public servant for my abilities. One of which is compassion. It's obviously something you only pretend to have. Now, show me to my sister."

"I've decided not to," the big woman spat.

"That wouldn't be wise." Michael interrupted from his spot by the window. "You see, we're under direct orders of the President himself."

"Really?"

"Really. And if you do anything that could cause Miss Schmidt any distress which would eventually lead to her failure to track down this man we're after, then I'm afraid you would have his office to answer to."

"Come on," she laughed. "I'm not going to fall for that. We all work for the President of the United States."

Michael shrugged. "Okay. Come on, Marin." He offered her his hand. "We'll let her find out the hard way. You can call

Karyn from the hotel room."

They began to walk out the door.

"Stop!" Harris boomed. "You swear you're working for him?"

"Directly. In fact, I was talking to him just this morning. Face to face."

She eased her way out of her chair, then decided not to stand. "The visiting area is down the hall and to your left."

"Thank you," Marin said without smiling.

"Thank you very much," Michael added. "We will remember this."

"I hope you do," the large woman added. "Heed my advice, Miss Schmidt."

"As far as I could throw you," Marin grumbled as Michael led her into the hallway. "The nerve of that woman!"

"Shh. She thought she was doing right. It's what the state tells her to do."

"I know. I know. Still—"

"Here we are."

They walked into the brightly painted room and waited. Karyn was brought in with her hands and feet shackled together. Her straight black hair lay over her face in a disheveled mess. She kept her head down so they could not see.

"Karyn?" Marin ran forward as soon as the guard left, lifting her sister's face in her hands.

Her beautiful, milky white complexion was mottled and blotchy. Her eyes were swollen and red, the rims of her eyelids tinged with black and blue.

"My god," Marin gasped. "What's happened to you?"

NINETEEN

JASON CULBERTSON HAD THE TYPICAL PHYSIQUE of a long distance runner, thin legs, slight torso. He looked anemic. Geoffrey Wallrich was relieved to see this as the other man walked quickly over the rise of the bridge.

He checked his watch. It was nearly eight o'clock and he had been waiting over three hours. He worked his way up the brick steps after Culbertson passed by the little park and followed the computer programmer around the corner to his apartment door, staying far enough behind so as not to be noticed.

His freshness and Culbertson's fatigue helped him as he rushed the other man.

Both of them fell into the steep flight of steps. Instantly, Wallrich heard barking, followed by a deep growl. He looked up into the darkening stairwell expecting a charging animal. When nothing happened, he kicked the door to and ordered Culbertson to shut the alarm off.

"Who are you?" the sweaty runner insisted as the dog continued to threaten.

"Shut it off!" Wallrich felt himself shaking as he reached for his gun and pressed it into the younger man's kidneys. "Now!"

"Dog alarm off!" his captive shouted.

Wallrich pulled himself up and grabbed Culbertson by the shirt. "Get up!"

167

Jason turned around in the wan light that made its way through the door's sheer curtains. "Who are you? Government?"

"Get upstairs." Wallrich waved the gun. He slowly felt his inhibitions giving away to aggression. Jason was quickly becoming the impersonal embodiment of everything he had hated and buried over his checkered career. "Now!"

The programmer moved slowly toward his apartment. Nervous sweat mixed with that of his recent exertion, mingling with the tears that were coursing down his cheeks. His mind raced for a way out of this situation. He entered the living room at the head of the stairs and looked frantically for something to hit his accoster with.

There was nothing.

He was not a violent person. Harming another human was always farthest from his mind.

Wallrich looked at the spartan room. "Where's the computer?"

"Back this way." He led the stranger toward the back bedroom and watched as the madman attempted to kick the door open. "Stop. Put that gun away. Just tell me what you want?"

"You know what I want, Bezalel," Wallrich cursed.

Jason felt his pulse quicken. His eyes grew wide. "Bezalel?"

"Yes. You know what I'm talking about, don't you?"

"Door open," Culbertson commanded.

The old wooden door hissed and slowly swung back into the room. Both men stepped cautiously across the threshold.

"Now, give me Adam," Wallrich growled as he pointed the gun toward Jason's head.

The younger man ran over to his operating chair and turned on his system. "It'll take a minute to boot," he said as he entered a secret prefix code into the command pad.

"Adam on line," the system announced.

Wallrich smiled as he looked around the room at the stacks

168

and stacks of processing units. "I imagine you could keep him in here if he wasn't running."

Culbertson smiled as he touched another code.

"Adam discontinued," the system announced. "Erasure complete in ten seconds. Nine...eight...."

Michael looked at his watch. It was nearly midnight and they had not come out of the emergency room yet. He shook his head as he thought about Marin. She had absolutely blown a fuse when she saw Karyn. It had been everything he could do to keep her from beating the guard up.

Her professionalism resurfaced quickly helping them get to the Miami Valley Medical Center. Karyn had been quickly brought under a physician's care, no thanks to the penal authorities. However, like in all medical facilities, the wait for results was excruciating.

He watched the television again, then rubbed his eyes and shut them. The day had been too long already. His reservations at the Holiday Inn were already confirmed and the charge for his rooms taken from his credit line, but it did not look as if he was going to need them after all.

"Michael?" He felt a gentle hand shaking his shoulder and realized with some embarrassment that he had fallen fast asleep.

He rubbed his eyes and blinked as Marin's cute face came into focus. She looked just as tired as he did, but fresher, better for the night.

He yawned. "How is Karyn?"

"Fine now." She moved over beside him. "You were really snoring away. You're exhausted."

"No." He sat up. "I didn't realize I snored. I'm all right."

"Did you ever get hold of Jason Culbertson?"

Michael grabbed his phone and hit the redial button. "No. I guess I forgot all about it. What's the matter with your sister?"

"Anemia. The baby made her worse. They're keeping her

here for a few days until they get her iron levels built back up. It's a good thing we stopped when we did. Those—"

Michael raised his hand as a voice answered the line.

"Culbertson residence," the slightly familiar voice said.

"Is Jason there?"

"Are you family?" The speaker's tone was somber.

"No. I'm a friend."

"Could I have your name, sir?"

"Krumm. Michael Krumm."

"Oh," the voice chuckled. "I thought it sounded like you. This is Doug McKinnon."

Michael put his hand over the pickup and whispered, "McKinnon's already there."

"What?" Marin frowned. "He was supposed—"

"We didn't hear from you." The Federal agent continued. "So I sent a team up here to investigate. They found Culbertson at his workstation."

"Is he all right?" Michael let himself ask, even though he knew the answer.

"No." McKinnon hesitated. "He's been shot. Lost a lot of blood."

"Who did it?"

"We're not sure yet, but we have a description of an older man. Whoever did it panicked and jumped out one of these windows. The police are checking area hospitals. The fellow might have broken his leg."

"We'll be there as soon as we can."

"Right. I'll wait for you."

"What's going on?" Marin grabbed his arm.

"Someone broke in on Jason and shot him." He stood up and stretched. "I've got to go."

"I'm coming with you. Just give me a minute to tell Karyn." She ran back to her sister's room returning within a few minutes. "Okay. She's sleeping."

"Must be nice."

When they reached the old house where Culbertson lived, it was cordoned off and surrounded by police cruisers, their lights flashing blue and purple against the adjacent buildings. A crowd of onlookers lined the plastic ribbons that acted as a fragile barrier. The local news reporters were broadcasting from the office building roof across the street.

Michael shook his head. It was apparent that Troy was unused to the excitement of an attempted murder. Or maybe it was McKinnon's helicopter sitting in the parking lot next to the river with its large Federal Bureau of Investigation emblem glowing in its own lights.

They showed their credentials to the local officer guarding the rope closest to the entrance. He looked at them suspiciously and raised his radio to his mouth.

"It's all right, Officer!" McKinnon shouted from the stoop in front of Culbertson's door. "They're with me. Let them pass."

Marin took her ID back and slipped it back into her pocket, reading the policeman's badge. "Thank you, Officer Bretland," she smiled. "Keep up the good work."

He gave her a half salute. "Officer Schmidt."

"What was that for?" Michael asked. Was there a little hint of jealousy in his voice? "No need to kiss up to the locals."

"Common courtesy." She yawned. "International brotherhood of law enforcement officers and all that." She looked at Culbertson's door. "You understand."

"Yes." Krumm sighed. "I understand."

She checked the frame and the lock latch as they entered the stairwell. "It wasn't a forced entry."

"No. We figure the perpetrator jumped him as he was entering the house. There is some evidence of a scuffle here at the base of the stairway. Forensics has detected a large amount of sweat on the carpet fibers on the first through fifth steps, as if Culbertson had been forced down."

"What about his workstation?" Michael asked as they

worked their way up into the apartment. He took in the musty smell of the old building. The windows were curtainless, only antiquated shutters guarded from an outside view. They were closed and secured at the moment to prevent prying eyes and lenses from seeing the interior of the dwelling.

McKinnon led them to the right and then through the door to Culbertson's office. Michael immediately walked over to the workstation and sat down behind the keypad.

"Sir!" a local inspector protested.

"He's has clearance, Robert," McKinnon said in an effort to impress Krumm and Schmidt with his authority.

"Yes, but he will be disturbing State's evidence."

"This thing won't get that far." Michael sighed as he hit a sequence that would call up the last thing the computer had done.

The screen flickered and then the words "Emergency Memory Dump" appeared. He then called up the hard disc which had been responsible for the action.

"What are you doing?" Marin asked as she casually took in the bloody mess under Michael's feet. There was a trail leading to the broken window at the room's northern corner.

"I'm going to find out what he dumped. There should be a file name left."

"Officer?" she asked the investigator. "Have your people checked the blood running to the window?"

"Yes," the man said as he pulled his pad from his pocket. "Your name?"

"Marin Schmidt. I'm an investigator with the Somerset County Sheriff's Department."

"That's New Jersey?"

"Yes. How did you know?"

"My grandfather used to live over there, near Milford. I spent my summers there as a boy."

She smiled. It was always good to run into someone who knew where home was.

He continued. "We did determine it's a different blood type than Mister Culbertson's. The guy may have shot himself. There's no evidence that he cut himself on anything. The blood is on the sidewalk below the window also."

"Where did the trail go?"

They walked over and looked out the window toward the far southern corner of the intersection of Market and Water Street. "He had a car parked right over there."

"Anyone see the car?"

"Yes. A sheriff's deputy saw a man park the vehicle and walk toward this building. He talked to the fellow. Said he looked out of place in his jeans and polo shirt. He was probably an executive type. Culbertson did a lot of contracting with businesses, designing programs and whatnot."

"Adam!" Michael yelled.

Marin ran back to his side. "What?"

"He dumped the Adam file." He swung the bloody chair around to face her. "Now who would be after that?" he whispered.

McKinnon perked up, pulling himself away from his conversation with another Federal agent. "You found something?"

"Yes." Michael looked at him defiantly. "Jason dumped the Adam file. What were you doing last night, Douglas?"

"Hey! Wait a minute! You don't think we had anything to do with this, do you?"

"It seems that the program was his attacker's goal. It also seems funny that you and your cronies were already here."

"We flew up from Dayton, Mike. You think we'd be stupid enough to land a helicopter in the middle of town, carry out an assassination attempt and then stick around and see if anyone could figure out if we did it or not?"

"I wouldn't put it past you."

Marin stepped between the two men before the situation could escalate. "Michael, calm down. Jason was your friend and you can't look at this objectively."

"Right," McKinnon asserted.

Marin turned away from Michael and put a hand on the agent's shoulder. "Shut up, Doug."

"Right," Michael leered.

"There were other people interested in recovering Adam," she said calmly as her thoughts recalled the figure she had seen sitting on the bench the evening before.

"Himmel," he answered.

"Oh my. Blast it!" she swore to herself.

"What?"

Her eyes were closed as she ran the scene over in her mind. The man. The balding head, thin features. "It was Geoffrey Wallrich I saw sitting on that park bench last night."

Michael's eyes widened then narrowed in unbelief. "He could do this?"

"He was fuming when he left my office the other day," she remembered out loud. "And what better way to get his job back than to recover Adam?"

Michael went back to the workstation and double-checked the files.

"What are you doing now?" she asked.

"I just want to make sure the files were indeed dumped and not transferred. If he got a copy of them—"

TWENTY

EVEN THOUGH HE WAS UNCONSCIOUS, JASON'S face was drawn in pain. The doctors had told them that the bullet had lodged next to his spinal cord after ricocheting off his ribs and puncturing one kidney and his liver. They had done the best they could to stop the internal hemorrhaging, their efforts only delayed the inevitable.

Michael sat with his chair pulled close to the edge of the bed. His hand barely touched Jason's. He tried talking to his childhood friend but found the words strained, choked and forced. No next of kin had been alerted to his fleeting state of health. There were none to alert.

Marin hugged herself as she stood in the far corner and watched Michael stare helplessly at his old friend. The whole thing was totally out of anyone's control.

On the way to the hospital he had finally explained to her the significance of his relationship to Jason Culbertson. It seems they had met early on in high school. Jason was a young man with very little hope for his future. His mother had died years before he and his father had moved to Troy. Shortly after that, his father had abandoned him. The state had allowed him to remain in foster care and continue in the public school system.

Michael had taken a liking to him during their sophomore year. Seeing that Jason had a case of bad self-esteem, he had sworn secretly to himself to help the orphan change his attitude about himself. It was not a particularly pious act on Michael's part, it was more an act of true friendship. He expected nothing in return.

Jason was particularly adept in the programming field and Michael taught him everything he knew. Throughout high school and even into the early college years, the pair designed games and special programs for those around them. But there had been a time when they had hacked their way into the school's, the state's and eventually the federal government's security files and records. They had made a small mint changing records for their peers.

It did not last long enough for any officials to notice and they had been very careful to wipe clean their footprints as they backed out of the deal. To this day it had been their secret and their unspoken tie that bound them until death.

Then Michael had been recruited by a large firm halfway through his first semester in college. It was a hard separation, especially for Jason. They lost touch for almost five years.

Michael had been the one to look Jason up after that long time. He was relieved to hear of his relative success with Dayton Data as a systems designer. From that point on, their friendship was rekindled, but never to the point it had been when they were boys.

Jason moaned and Michael grabbed his hand. "Jason? It's me Michael."

"Krumm?" the other's voice rasped. "I knew you'd be here."

"Sorry about all this." Michael tried to hold back the tears that were already burning his cheeks.

Jason coughed as he tried to shrug. "Did they get him?"

"The guy that shot you?"

"No. Adam. Is he—?"

"He's gone, Jason." Michael looked up at Marin and she stepped out into the hall to get McKinnon. "You did well."

"You'd have done the same for me." He squeezed Michael's hand as best he could. The pressure was very weak. "I did as you asked."

"I know. I only wish now that I hadn't asked."

"Hey. No regrets here. I was getting tired of life anyway." He closed his eyes and drew in a painful breath. "You know how lonely it is. Everybody wants a piece of you..."

"...but nobody wants you," Michael finished for him. "Yeah. I'm still going down that road."

Douglas McKinnon entered the room quietly, his recorder extended. "Mister Culbertson, I'm Douglas McKinnon with the National Bioethics Advisory Committee. We're investigating the Himmel programming using the human genome."

Jason waved his hand. "I know what you're after." He looked at Michael and smiled. "Himmel doesn't have it, I don't have it and you guys will never get it."

"The Adam Program," McKinnon stated for the record.

"Adam," Culbertson confirmed.

"Then you are Bezalel." McKinnon's voice was shaking a little.

Jason closed his eyes. "I have used that pseudonym to fulfill contracts."

"Thank you." Douglas closed the contact on his recorder and shoved the device back into his jacket pocket. "I'm sorry it had to come to this."

"Just catch the idiot who shot me. He's running scared."

He pulled out a picture of Wallrich from another pocket. "This the man?"

Jason shook his head as his body was racked by another coughing fit. McKinnon looked at Marin and then at Michael and frowned in confusion as he backed out of the room. It was hard to trust the judgment of someone in that much pain. Geoffrey Wallrich was as good as caught.

"He didn't see anything." Jason managed to laugh. "I hit the dump command before the system was fully booted. All the programming notes, everything. Of course," he wheezed, "the guy who shot me didn't see it either."

"A complete wipe," Michael affirmed, missing his friend's reference to his assailant. "I even double-checked for anything that might have been cross stored. You left no residuals."

"You taught me well, Master," Culbertson mocked.

"I told you never to call me that." Krumm feigned frustration. "Weed hopper."

"And I told you never to call me that." Jason gasped. "Oh that hurts. Thanks for—"

He took in a deep breath and held it for an incredibly long time. Michael watched his old friend in disbelief as he attempted to sit up.

"I'm getting out of here!" Jason said as he threw the bed sheets off his body. A pool of blood had formed on the bed below his right side. "I'm okay!"

Then, as suddenly as he had sat up, he fell back in a relaxed heap. His lips moved slightly.

Michael leaned over close to him.

Jason smiled then frowned. His brown eyes questioning what he was seeing. "Mom?"

Michael laid his head down on his friend's chest and cried.

Marin remained at the end of the bed and watched. Only when he had finished mourning the loss of his friend did she put her arms around him and hold him.

Kyle Pierce looked out of the video monitor at his former associate. His hair had been jumbled and pressed flat by the silk sheets of his bed, destroying his controlled good looks. "Wallrich?" he cursed in a scratchy voice.

"I thought I fired him?" a groggy female voice said from behind him.

"I found Bezalel." Geoffrey laughed at the former CEO. "I found him in Troy, Ohio."

Pierce finally woke up enough to realize what the scientist

was talking about. His mind was still foggy with the previous evening's exploits. "Did you get the program back?"

Wallrich hung his head and then looked back up at the screen. "No. Kyle, I'm leaving the country."

"What? Geoff, what did you do?" He pulled the sheets around him, uncovering his partner.

Wallrich got an embarrassed glimpse of his former boss's backside as she scrambled for the floor.

"What did you do!" Pierce screamed.

"There was a scuffle." The researcher tried to remain calm. "He tried to destroy the files. I was going to kill him, but someone else came in on us. He shot me in the arm before I jumped out the window and ran." He looked warily from right to left. "I'm all right though. It's just a nick. I had no choice, Kyle."

"You did have a choice. You went in on him armed?"

Silence. Wallrich's face had disappeared.

"Geoffrey?"

"I'm still here."

"Where are you? I'll send a car."

Wallrich leaned back into the picture. "I'm at Kennedy. I'll be on my way to—" He stopped.

"Where?" Kyle asked as he picked up another phone and dialed the FBI.

"No, Kyle. I'm not that stupid. They'll be looking for me." He looked around. "I'll be checking in with you in a month or two."

Lynda Swicknagl crawled up over the edge of the bed, behind Pierce. "If he gets away, Himmel will be implicated."

Kyle waved her off as he handed her the other phone. She reached forward and pinched his one bare buttock.

"You're not stupid, Geoff. No one else was able to catch the guy. Listen, I'll talk to Lynda and see if she'll reconsider the acceptance of your resignation."

"You're stalling now, Kyle." His voice became suddenly

drained. "I've got to go."

"No!" He picked up the transceiver and shook it as if it were Wallrich himself. "Geoff, wait!"

The screen went blank.

Pierce put the extension down and looked over at Lynda. She grinned. "They're on their way."

"Great." Pierce climbed back into bed. "Now where were we?"

"I think I was about to get out of bed," she said. "I'm going to have a busy day tomorrow and so are you."

"But we were about to—" he pleaded.

"I am no longer in the mood," she snapped. "That's always been your shortcoming, Kyle. You're insensitive to women." She walked into the bathroom and turned on the water. "But I guess that's not your fault. I never met a man who could think beyond his libido."

He rubbed his hair and realized how it must have looked to Wallrich. It was only then that he truly panicked. The scandal of Kyle Pierce seen with hairs out of place. He almost couldn't bear it.

"Mind if I join you in there?" he called to Zwicknagl.

"Not at all," she chimed back. "I need someone to do my back anyway."

They stayed in Troy for another three days. Michael saw to Jason's funeral and to the safekeeping of his equipment, while Marin took time to make sure her sister would never again fall into such pitiful shape. Karyn was looking like a vibrant china doll now and her big sister wanted to keep it that way.

They drove back to the penal facility under the watchful eye of one guard in Marin's rented car. Karyn had reclined her seat so she could look out the sunroof as they talked. "So what are you going to tell Mother?"

"The truth." Marin turned onto Eldean Road. "I can't keep anything from her. You of all people know that."

"Yeah," Karyn sighed as she reached up toward the small opening in the car's ceiling, grasping at the narrow rays of sunlight that pierced through the maple trees as they crossed the Miami River. "I actually wish she had been able to come with you this time."

Marin looked over at her sister and frowned. "What are you driving at, sis? You two hate each other."

"Oh no, we don't." Karyn smiled. "We hate what we do to each other, but now I'm carrying this fetus, I—well, I don't know. I feel different somehow." She ran her warm hand through her silky black hair and then patted the spot on her stomach just below her navel. "I feel connected to womanhood suddenly."

"Oh, knock the melodrama off," Marin coughed. "You won't get through to me like that. Life's just a big game to you. People are parts that can be moved and played with. You're not connected to anything. You never have been."

"I don't know, Marin," she responded calmly as she twisted her hair around her index finger. "Maybe it's the hormones or something."

"Yeah. Or maybe those pain killers are still working."

"You don't give painkillers to a pregnant woman," she protested. "It could harm the baby."

"We don't want that." She tried to think of the day when she would hold the child in her arms and take responsibility for it. Then Karyn would be free again, free to get pregnant at the drop of a hat if she wished. Would she take that child also?

"What about Michael?" Karyn asked out of the blue.

"What about him? He's pretty upset about his friend dying."

"No. Not that. You like him, don't you?"

Marin felt her face grow warm as she blushed. "Yes, but he's a California-type person. He's really important."

"And you're not."

"No. I don't think it could ever work out. There are some things about him that bother me. He's got a dark side to him."

"And you don't?"

"I don't think I do."

"When was the last time you wanted to shoot a rapist in the head?"

"What? Never!"

"You mean to tell me you have never been filled with so much rage that you would disregard everything moral that you hold dear just to get even, just to deal justice in your own special way?"

Marin did not answer right away. There had been occasions when she had to pull herself out of a situation and run from the temptation to use violence for her own benefit. There were also the times she had left the courtroom almost nauseated because of the lack of justice she had seen dealt.

She slammed on the brakes as a horrible thought gushed up from her subconscious. "My god!" she gasped.

Karyn raised her seat and looked at her sister. Marin had placed her right index fingernail in her mouth and was vigorously chomping away at it. Her gaze was directed toward the dashboard, but it was unfocused.

"Stop it, Marin." Karyn managed a whisper as the guard leaned forward. "You're scaring me."

Then just as quickly as it had hit her, the fit dissipated. She rubbed her forehead and looked back at the guard. The young woman looked back at her, unsure of whether to go for her gun or get out.

Marin pushed hard on the accelerator. "Mind if we take a little side trip?"

TWENTY-ONE

SHE PULLED INTO THE DRIVEWAY OF Culbertson's apartment and jumped out of the car, leaving her sister with the guard. Officer Bretland met her at the door then let her pass as soon as he recognized her. Other than a few forensics people and some stray blue suited officers, the apartment was abandoned. The chief investigator had done his job and was now waiting for the microscopic information that would confirm his deductions.

Fortunately, the crime scene was still being documented and none of the evidence had been removed. Marin stopped at the door to Jason's office.

"Something wrong, ma'am?" Bretland asked as he followed her.

She looked around the room. The blood where Jason had fallen and the blood on the broken windowsill were as she remembered them, but she looked at it from a different angle this time. Why she had not returned after Jason had died escaped her. She rubbed her scalp. He had clearly said that there had been another man and that Wallrich had not shot him.

McKinnon had ignored it. Michael had ignored it. She had let it fly right over her head. She got down on her hands and knees and crawled over to the blood marks. She looked up, taking in the splatter from the bullet's penetration. The smeared floor, blood on the edge of the table and a small crescent at the

183

edge of the dried up puddle next to the spot where the gun had been laid down on the floor, its barrel pointing toward the office door.

She reached over and grabbed Bretland's revolver. He protested until he realized what she was going to do. She stood near the crescent shape, lining her foot up with the edge of it. It put her body perpendicular to the seat Jason had used. She then extended her arm in a perfect firing stance. Then she dropped the gun and tried to run toward the window.

The gun bounced off the back of the chair and landed next to the wall. The other officers gathered around and watched as she did it five more times, each time with the chair at a slightly different angle. Each time the gun landed against the far wall and her exit toward the window had been blocked by the chair.

She handed the gun back to Bretland and squatted down to examine to floor again. Whoever had shot Jason had stood next to him for a long time before leaving. Long enough for his blood to run up against the edge of their shoe. She stood up again and asked for the forensics people to come in and spray for bloodstains running toward the door.

After a few minutes, in black light, similar crescents were revealed. They moved evenly out the door until they faded shortly before reaching the steps.

"Now, perhaps you'll explain," Bretland asked as he withdrew his recorder.

Marin looked at him. "Whoever killed Jason Culbertson enjoyed watching him die." She took another step toward the stairway and shook her head. The head researcher at Himmel had impressed her as a man dedicated solely to his calling. Violence did not fit his personality at all. "It wasn't Geoffrey Wallrich. That's probably his blood splattered on the wall by the window."

"Then who?" He held the flat pad-like device closer to her.

"I'm not sure, but Michael probably wasn't far from the mark."

Bretland frowned. He had missed the confrontation between Krumm and McKinnon and he would have to miss the next one too.

She left her sister and the guard equally confused when she finally said her good-byes an hour later.

"I still don't understand what that was all about," Karyn said as she hugged her. "You've lost it, haven't you?"

"No." Marin hugged her sister back. "It's my job," she smiled. "The subconscious mind works all the time. I'd seen things and heard things that, in the trauma of the event, didn't register."

"Until we were talking about something completely different."

"Yes."

"Just like those nights when you would sit bolt upright in bed and then run to your drawing table or canvas and draw something that seemed totally unimportant."

Marin grinned in embarrassment. She'd forgotten about those days when her art was the most important thing to her. "Yeah." She laughed. "Same thing."

"You ever going to paint again?" Karyn shoved her hands in her pockets. "I liked your paintings."

"Yeah, you sold everyone I ever gave you."

"And even some you didn't." She shrugged. "I needed the money."

"More lost children." Marin shook her head. "I don't know. I tell myself I'll pick the brushes up again, but something always gets in the way."

"Yeah." Karyn patted her belly. "I'm afraid I'll be ruining any future hope for that."

"Don't think of it that way. The baby will be yours to adopt after you get straightened out."

The younger Schmidt laughed. "Yeah, right. I don't think that will ever be."

"You're young yet. Funny things happen to people after

185

they turn thirty. You've got a few years yet."

"What's thirty got to do with it?"

Marin shook her head again. "I don't know. I just started viewing life a little differently then. I started feeling like I was my own mother."

"Don't tell me that." She came over and hugged Marin one last time before reentering the gate. "I love you, sis. Thanks."

"Same here. You take care of yourself and I'll see you in December or January." Mist shrouded her eyes.

Then they were through the gates and gone from sight. Marin leaned on the hood of her rent-a-car for a long time before climbing back into it and heading south. "All those lost children," she said to herself. "And all those that will never be."

Douglas McKinnon was no longer in Dayton. He had flown back to Washington as soon as he heard of Geoffrey Wallrich's capture at Kennedy International. The scientist insisted he did not murder Culbertson. He admitted to the assault and the intent to harm the young programmer, but he insisted he could not bring himself to do it.

McKinnon looked over the report again as the President slurped at his cup of coffee.

"We can nail this guy for the murder," he said without question.

"Oh yes, sir. The FBI has given us assurance of that." He laid the folio down on the President's desk. "But the story of the other man bothers me."

"Ah." Gates waved the agent's concerns off. "Fiction. He's trying to save his own hide."

"I'm going up to New York and talk to him myself. I was at the crime scene."

"Yes. Go ahead," the Chief Executive gave him permission. "That's not the reason I called you here, though. I want to know if this Culbertson guy was our man."

186

"I have little doubt that he was the one, sir," McKinnon smiled.

"Good." Gates took another drink. "Then we can consider this case closed?"

"Your reputation is still sound, sir, and no one has Adam."

"Or his builder."

"Yes, sir." He moved toward the door.

"What about this Krumm fellow? Could he build us a cyber-human?"

Douglas shrugged. "If he's as good as they say he is, I would think so."

Gates smiled and turned to look out the window of the Oval Office at the grey fortress-like walls that protected him from the world. "Perhaps that is something we should consider then."

"Perhaps, sir." He opened the door. "Good day, sir."

The President waved his hand and pushed his hair back into place. "Perhaps a virtual president in my image."

Michael spread the black dirt over the edge of the grave with his hands and cursed himself again. Jason's death had been unnecessary. Unnecessary. He felt the hot tears rolling down his face once again. It was all his fault.

"I'm sorry, Jason," he choked. "If I'd known it was going to lead to this—"

"We must all die, Mister Krumm." A stranger's voice interrupted from behind him. "His death was not significant."

Michael turned around to see a thin man with short cropped black hair staring at him from the next plot over. "It's significant to him and to me." He stood up making eye contact with the stranger. "Who are you? How do you know my name?"

The man shoved his hands in his loose fitting trousers and walked closer to him. Michael kept a wary eye on him. His sharp features did not speak favorably of him. The deep-set eyes looked intelligent, but evil. And that long ratty string of hair that fell down the middle of his back told of an antisocial view to life.

"Who are you?" Michael demanded again.

"Let's say I'm a follower of yours and your consort's." His smile was dry.

"Consort?" Michael stepped back unconsciously.

"The good Detective Schmidt."

"Marin? Why? Are you following—" His thoughts suddenly snapped back to Marin's creepy description of Hugh Rache, the mass murderer she had put behind bars. "Rache?" he managed.

"Marin Schmidt has done me a great disservice, Mister Krumm." Rache smiled. "I detest being locked away like a common animal." He spat as he moved toward Michael. "I also detest being caught by a woman. If you were any kind of a man, Mister Krumm, you would convince her that a professional career is a big mistake. She should leave her line of work up to the men of the world."

Michael frowned at the convicted killer. His heart was racing, but he was doing everything within his power to convey calmness and strength. "Is that why you killed all those women?"

"I did not kill anyone." He continued to smile. "They killed themselves. A woman's place is in the home. Many men have suffered because women have taken their position in the work force. When they should be home and subservient to their male masters."

"Ah." Michael managed a chuckle. "Hugh, you're getting a little melodramatic now. That's not the way Marin described you."

"Oh? How did the great detective paint her victim?"

"She said you were conniving, underhanded, clever, a coward."

Rache's face flushed. "A coward? How dare she!"

"You never looked your victims in the face. You poisoned

them. Stabbed them in the back, so to speak." Michael started moving slowly toward his car. "A real man would look his victim in the eye."

"I'm no longer like that, Michael." He grinned as he stepped in Michael's path. "I watched your friend die. I didn't poison him either. I looked him straight in the eye as I fired the other man's gun at him and as the blood oozed from his body."

"You killed him?"

"I just said that, didn't I? Yes. I believe I did."

"And now you intend to kill me."

"No. Not yet. I want Marin first." He walked over to the car. "I intend for you to take me to her."

"And if I don't." Michael felt ever muscle in his body begin to shake as the fear of the moment finally overtook him.

"You love life too much." Rache pulled a small revolver from his pants pocket.

"Get in the car."

Michael sighed with frightened disgust.

"Thank you," the murderer smiled. "You don't know how much I appreciate this."

As Michael slid into the driver's seat, he punched in the ignition code and revved the motor up. Rache grabbed the doorframe and carefully pulled his body into the passenger seat.

Michael did not wait until Rache was fully in before slamming the drive into gear. The wheels chirped against the pavement as the doors slammed into place. Rache screamed as his hand became lodged in the doorframe. He aimed the gun at Michael's head and pulled the trigger.

The plastic by his left ear shattered as Rache took aim again. By this time Michael was screaming as he punched the brake peddle and the door release at the same time.

Another shot was fired taking out the front windshield.

Rache yelled even louder as he found himself being carried forward by the sudden stop. His hand ripped free of the doorframe and he rolled out in front of the car. Michael gunned the motor again and felt the car ride over what he thought was Rache.

Another hole exploded in the window next to him as he rounded the wide curve that would lead him out of the cemetery and to safety.

He picked up his phone and dialed the police but it crackled lifelessly in his hand. A stray bullet had hit it.

He couldn't remember where the police station was so he headed in the general direction of downtown Troy. However, before he had even crossed the river, blue lights were flashing in his rearview mirror and a squad car was ordering him over to the side of the street.

He stopped and jumped out of the car.

Two officers opened their doors and came out with their pistols drawn. "Michael Krumm?" the driver asked.

"Yes."

"Hit the ground. Hands out to your side."

"What? I was just coming to get you guys! There's a man in the cemetery. He just tried to kill me."

The first officer ran forward and grabbed him by the wrist while the other leveled his weapon at his head and order him to shut up.

"You're under arrest for the murder of Jason Culbertson," the first officer was saying as he snapped a pair of handcuffs down hard on Michael's wrists. "You have the right to remain silent. Anything you say can and will be used against you in a court of law."

"You idiots! There is a mass murderer loose and you arrest me!" he screamed as they lifted him from the ground and dragged him over to their vehicle. "He's the one who did it. Go to the cemetery. I ran over him."

"Right," the second officer smiled. "Now shut your mouth." He reached in the car and pushed Michael's head into the seat. "Not another word until we get to the station."

Michael tried to ignore the sweaty smell of the squad car's back seat as he lay there humiliated. His mind raced. What could have brought this on? Who was the moron in charge of this investigation? Where was Marin?

What if Rache found her?

He already knew the answer to that.

"Come on, guys," he protested. "Just once around the cemetery."

"I said shut your mouth," the second officer repeated as his hand landed hard against the back of Michael's head with a resounding crack. "Next time you'll feel my billy stick."

"Idiot," Michael growled.

TWENTY-TWO

MARIN STOPPED BY THE HOTEL TO check on Michael before she made her way back to the police station to discuss her theories with the detective in charge of the investigation of Jason's murder. She could not get the government conspiracy thought out of her mind until she talked to the investigator and McKinnon. The fact that a second man had been involved freed Wallrich from suspicion, even though he accosted Culbertson with the intent to do him harm.

But why would the Feds want Jason dead? Sure the incident had been an embarrassment to Gates. However, that was not a good enough reason. Abducting Jason was more along the lines of current government policy, she thought. Abducting him and forcing him to do for Uncle Sam what he had done for Himmel.

She reached the third floor of the hotel and walked the short distance to Michael's room. She could easily see his door was standing wide open from the stairs, but she thought nothing of it. It was a mild day and the air seemed crisp and fresh. He was the kind of person who preferred natural air to conditioned air.

"Michael?" she called out before she reached the door. "Michael."

There was no response. Her pace slowed as her law enforcement instincts automatically kicked in.

"Michael!" she called again. Nothing.

Her hand went to the spot under her arm where her pistol

should have been. She mumbled a low curse. She was out of her jurisdiction and had not brought the gun. She stopped and peered around the edge of the doorframe. Then she pulled her head back and moved away, back toward the stairs. She had seen enough.

His room had been torn to pieces. Clothing and papers had been scattered everywhere. The bed covers had been torn and the mattresses carelessly tossed against the wall. She had seen no blood, no sign that he had been there when the break-in had occurred. Someone had been looking for something.

She made her way to the hotel lobby and reported the room to the manager before calling the police. Then she showed the woman behind the desk her credentials and ordered her to close and lock the room until the police arrived.

She looked at Marin as if she were crazy.

"What's the matter?"

"Oh nothing, ma'am." The other woman looked at the New Jersey state seal on Marin's badge. "It's just that the police were just here. I gave them the key to the room when they showed me the warrant."

"Warrant?"

"Yes." The manager brushed a lock of curly brown hair away from her eyes. "They said they had reason to believe the room was occupied by the very man who murdered that Culbertson fellow. I had no choice."

"And my room?"

"The warrant just had Mister Krumm's name on it." She smiled, finally feeling as if she had done something right. "They didn't touch your stuff. I wouldn't let them."

"Well, thank you." Marin turned and left the lobby.

Her brakes squealed as she pulled into a vacant space in front of the police station. The nose of the car missed the power jack by two feet. She flung the door open and charged past a group of officers.

"Can I help you?" one of them asked.

"You've done enough," she blurted out as she disappeared through the swinging doors.

"Hold it!" The captain behind the desk stopped her. "The fire station is two blocks down."

"Very funny, Captain. Where's the imbecile in charge of investigating the Culbertson murder?"

"Lieutenant Proudfit? He's in a meeting."

"Where?" She started past the desk.

"Hold it, lady. You can't just charge into this station like you own it."

She pulled her Federal agent papers out and flashed them in his face. "This was my case to begin with. You just sit there and watch me."

He raised his hands as his face paled with frustration. "Feds. Second floor, room twelve."

She darted up the marble staircase and charged down the hallway until she found the proper room. She knocked once then opened the door. A heavyset, balding fellow looked up at her with beady red-rimmed eyes. "What is the meaning of this?" he shouted.

"Marin Schmidt." She entered and took a seat as she eyed the other two men in the room with him. They were obviously FBI agents. "I'm with the Bioethics Advisory Commission."

"You're the one who turned me onto the second murderer," he smiled.

"I did? Is that why you've torn Michael Krumm's room to shreds?"

He looked at the other two Federal agents and nodded. "I'll have the paperwork in order by tonight, gentlemen." He interrupted her. "You can take the prisoner. Just show the turnkey this receipt."

Neither man said a word in reply as they stood and took the documentation they had been discussing and left.

Marin had no choice but to scoot her chair aside as they walked out the door.

Proudfit mustered a toothy smile after the door was closed again. "They're after a Federal suspect," he answered her unasked question. "Big time. The President himself sent them."

"Big deal," she sighed as she moved to one of the other previously occupied chairs. "Now what is this about me pointing you to a second murderer? And tearing Michael's room up."

He rubbed his nose. "Yes. Officer Bretland played me the tape of you looking over the murder scene again. I was quite intrigued, especially when you determined the path and stance of the other person. Very Holmesian. I must congratulate you."

"Oh, it was always there. Everyone was looking for one person, the one who jumped out the window." She ran her hands through her hair and then clutched them together in front of her. "I didn't notice the inconsistencies until I was away from it."

"Like I said, very Holmesian," he smiled greedily. "We have a good idea who the other man was."

She narrowed her eyes. "You think Michael Krumm did it, don't you?"

He pooched his lower lip out and shrugged. "Everything points to him. He and Culbertson were colleagues in some, let's call it techno-piracy when they were younger. There is no reason to believe the relationship did not continue in that light."

"So what's the motive?" She fought to remain calm. It would take very little for her to lose whatever semblance of control she still had. This guy was grasping for straws, trying to show up the Feds.

Proudfit shrugged again. "Culbertson was about to reveal something that Krumm didn't want known. Krumm finds out about it, comes to Troy, follows this Wallrich guy into the apartment, eavesdrops on the argument and grabs the gun before Wallrich can use it, forces the other guy out the window then shoots Culbertson."

"Feasible," Marin admitted.

"Thank you."

"Except he was with me the whole time! You dolt!" She slammed her hands down on his desk. "We came to Troy looking for Culbertson on Federal business. At the time of the murder we were in Piqua visiting my sister at the Woman's Penal Center. You can call and check their logs, if you like. Or do you just accuse people around here on conjecture alone?"

"Wha—" He stuttered. "I was just—"

"Just playing Sherlock Holmes? This is reality, mister! This is not one of your nineteenth-century detective novels! Now where is Michael? I want to see him."

Proudfit rubbed the back of his neck. "I was going on some reliable information. It came directly from the FBI. They swore out the warrant for him. We acted on their call."

"Whoa. You're now telling me you arrested him?"

"Yes."

"But not on any information you have obtained so far."

"Well—"

"And you tried to make it sound as if you were the genius behind this. You're less than a dolt. You're an imbecile. An idiot. A brainless—"

"I get the point," he groaned.

She stopped and crossed her arms. "Is he here?"

"Not anymore."

"What do you mean? You arrested him."

"On a Federal warrant. They have him now. Those two agents that just left have taken him."

"Where?"

"I don't know." He stood up and then sat back down, not sure what to do. "Probably to Wright-Patterson Air Force Base. It's the closest Federal installation besides the workfare offices."

She gritted her teeth together and attempted to reach over the desk for his neck. "No," she said as she stood back up and took a deep breath. "No. If the Feds have him there's only one place and one person who would be greedy enough to want him taken."

"Who's that?"

"The President."

"You're going after the President over this?"

She turned and walked through the doorframe slamming the door behind her. "Why not?"

As she descended the stairs her mind rolled with scenarios for Michael's arrest. Gates was not stupid and he knew what he wanted. Michael would be ordered to build an Adam model just as Jason had.

She stopped and smiled to herself as her gaze fell instinctively on the fugitive postings, an old habit, knowing Michael as she did he would do everything in his power not to grant Gates' wish. Her eyes stopped on the hard features of one of the criminals at large. His penetrating stare was still fresh in her mind. She could almost see him winking at her across the courtroom again.

"Oh no!" she gasped. "How in the—"

Marin picked up the nearest phone and dialed her office. The line buzzed until a familiar voice answered the hail. "Somerset County Sheriff's Department. Please state your emergency."

"Kevin?"

"Marin? Where are you?"

"In Troy, Ohio."

"We've been trying to get hold of you for days. You know he escaped."

"I just found out. How long ago?"

"Five days, a week ago." Kevin Neal went silent for a moment. "You better watch your back."

"No idea where he went?"

"None. They're not even sure when he disappeared. He's a smart guy."

"I know." She tapped her teeth with her fingertip. "Listen, watch my apartment. I'll be home tonight sometime. I'm sure he'll be coming after me."

"We already have two unmarkeds posted."

"Good. Bye." She hung the phone up and ran out to her car.

Michael's hotel room was locked and sealed with a long strip of yellow police department tape. She shoved the key card into her door slot and hurried in to gather her things. If she had any hope of catching up to the FBI agents she had to get on the highway as quickly as she could. Hopefully her Federal status still carried enough weight to get her onto the Air Force base and on the same plane they would be carrying Michael away in.

She grabbed her sparse collection of suits off the hanger and did a quick glance around the bathroom. There was nothing amiss. The bed had been remade and her toiletry items stacked in a neat pile by the sink. She scooped them into her bag and forced her clothes in on top of them. Then she headed back toward the door.

"What is the hurry, Detective Schmidt?" a cool voice asked from the shadowy corner by the window.

She dropped her bag and backed away. A quick look at the door told her he had locked the dead bolt and chained it while she had been flying around.

"Stupid!" she said silently to herself. "Stupid, stupid, stupid."

She looked at Hugh Rache through the dim reflected light from the bathroom. His eyes were like black coals, cold but full of energy.

Energy that would kill her.

TWENTY-THREE

AS HER EYES ADJUSTED TO THE dim backlight, she noticed he was holding his right hand carefully in his lap and that his face was scraped badly. In the other hand he held a small revolver.

"I've been wanting to talk to you," he growled from his seat. "I've been wanting to meet you ever since my arrest." He inhaled deeply through his nose. "But I didn't know who you were until the hearing. I'm glad you came to that. It saved me a lot of work. Though I would have found you eventually."

She moved slowly toward the door.

"I would not." He smiled. "You're a very busy person. You should rest."

Marin looked toward the windows hidden by the curtains. They were probably unbreakable. She would kill herself diving into one. The door was the only way out.

He leveled the gun at her head. "I think you need to take the weight off your feet. Lie down on the bed."

She frowned. "Rape isn't part of your M.O., Rache." Her voice quivered as she snapped back.

"Don't flatter yourself," he coughed. "Using a gun isn't part of my Motus Operendi either, but it didn't take much for me to use one on Krumm's friend."

"You killed him? Why? You didn't even know him."

"No, but he knew Michael Krumm and you were with him.

199

I needed a way to insure you would remain in Troy." He shrugged. "I came here to kill him anyway. The squirrelly little fellow from Himmel just gave me an advantage. I didn't have the means to travel to California. Now, lie down on the bed."

She hesitated then sat down on the edge farthest from him. "Why not wait for me in New Jersey?" she asked as her mind desperately raced for a plan to escape.

"You of all people should know I am not a moron. I'm highly intelligent and I have many sources. Friends. I've known your every move since you left New Jersey. I even knew enough to plan this lure of sorts."

She shrugged her shoulders in concession. "Yes. I'll concede to that. I would never have caught you if I hadn't found the right witness."

"The notorious street urchin." He shifted in the chair. "Lie down!"

"The eyes of justice are everywhere."

"Yes. So I've heard. Well, his eyes see nothing now. I considered him as a first order of business."

"Life means nothing to you, does it?"

"Oh, my life does. And my society." He lowered the gun briefly as he leaned toward her and whispered, "You know the world isn't quite right? I aim to change that. It's my mission."

"Killing professional women."

"Ridding the market place of intruders." He put the barrel of the gun against her forehead. "One last time. Lie down!"

She had no choice. She examined his hand as she lowered herself to the bed. Blood oozed from the makeshift bandage.

"Good." He rose to his feet. "Now be so kind as to unbutton your blouse and expose your arm."

She felt a cold sweat break out all over her body. She was becoming a victim and it scared her to death. She did not like it. "You won't get away with this."

"Sure I will. Your secret drug habit is about to catch up with you."

"I don't have—"

He leaned over her. His breath was horrid, like rotten fish. "You will."

She turned her head. "Why not stab me in the butt like your other victims?"

"Oh," he smiled as he gingerly placed the pistol in his wounded hand, "don't be silly. They were all nameless nobodies. You, on the other hand, have a great reputation to soil. 'The Great Detective Who Caught the Greatest Mass Murderer of the Twenty First Century.'"

His free hand slid into his pocket and pulled out a tiny syringe. Amber fluid glistened in the refracted light from the small split in the curtains behind him. "They won't know exactly what it was that killed you, but this will give indications of nicotine use, cocaine, heroin and alcohol. It'll make you look as if you were really screwed up. And to think, you hid it so well from those around you." He wagged his head with mock pity as he removed the protective cap.

Marin frowned. "I can't believe I'm just lying here letting you get away with this."

"It gives me great satisfaction to see it." His eyes brightened. "I'll rape you just before you die. I want you to know that. I've just got to add that one little element of immorality to your failed life," he snickered. "There will be a little sting."

The silence was shattered by the phone bleating loudly from its stand between the beds.

Rache looked at her and pulled back on the hammer of his gun. He winced with pain as he did it. "Who knows you're here?"

"The police. The front desk. A whole lot of people. If I don't answer it—"

"Do it, but remember, I'll be right behind you with the gun and the needle."

She moved over and picked the transceiver up. "Hello?"

The voice on the other end was distinctively Michael's. "Is your life in eminent danger?" he asked in a whisper.

"Yes," she said as she felt the point of the needle press against the skin of her neck. "I plan on checking out in a few minutes."

"Get down." The phone line clicked into silence as the room's picture windows exploded in a spray of automatic gunfire.

She covered her head and moved away from Rache. The room filled with his screams as bullets pierced his body. His pistol fired hitting her in the shoulder. As the needle punched into her skin, he fell away. She pulled it out as quickly as she could. Her head began to spin as nausea washed over her.

"No," she cursed as she fell the rest of the way to the floor.

The two agents she had seen in Proudfit's office climbed through the open window and surrounded the moaning Rache.

Marin fought to sit up.

Rache watched her as he remained motionless at the FBI agent's mercy. "Maybe next time," he croaked.

Michael came through the broken glass and bounced over the top of the bed. He quickly grabbed Marin under the arms and hoisted her up. "You all right?"

She found speaking to be a struggle. "I've been shot and drugged."

"Drugged?"

"With this." She showed him the compact needle and syringe. "I-I don't know what is doing what. I feel awful."

"An ambulance is on the way," he said softly as he tore a pillow case off a pillow and wrapped it around her bleeding arm. "You're going to be fine."

Rache laughed at the couple. "She'll be dead in a week."

Marin looked at the syringe and then at Rache. "I'll outlive you."

"No." He continued to giggle. "I'm not mortally wounded. I'll be back in jail, but I have many friends. Many friends. I

202

will find you again."

One of the agents moved over to her side. "May I have the drug, ma'am. We'll need it as evidence."

She handed him the vile and watched through fading vision as he walked back over by his partner. The sound of sirens grew louder. She looked at Michael and kissed him on the cheek before the room faded from her view.

Marin looked down from the jetliner's window at the rainy tarmac as they maneuvered into the terminal. She thought she could see the bulky figure of Sheriff Hutchinson and a couple of deputies staring through the foggy glass of the gate. He turned to give the other men orders, orders silenced by the barriers of glass, plastic and distance.

Her arm trembled as she tried to make it work. The bullet from Rache's pistol had damaged her elbow beyond repair, shattering it like an eggshell. She had had to have a replacement implanted. There were still weeks of therapy ahead.

The plane rocked to a stop and the pilot droned his gratefulness to the passengers for choosing his airline. He gave the local temperature and the weather forecast for the day before wishing them all well. She barely heard him.

She looked back out the window. It was all like a bad dream. Weeks had been spent in pursuit of a thief. The papers and her superiors called her successful, but Marin felt otherwise. The investigation had cost the life of an innocent man and nearly cost her her own. It had also brought her an inkling of feeling in love.

Michael's face flashed across her memory. She had not seen him or heard from him since the hotel room. That had been two weeks ago. She felt totally abandoned. Alone.

And now she would have to try to put her life back together, get back into the routine of being an investigator for Somerset County. Hours would be spent looking for the mundane criminals, for the occasional Hugh Raches who decided for themselves a judgment on their society. On her society.

But still, there was the memory of Michael and painting, Karyn and life unborn. And poor Adam, the virtual man she had known yet never met. Where was he? It was hard for her to believe that Jason Culbertson would simply destroy something, someone he had worked so hard to build. Even God gave his creation a second chance.

"There she is." She heard the familiar voice of her boss bellow through the open hatch.

She looked around. The cabin had emptied completely and she had not even noticed.

"Welcome back, Marin!" The sheriff smiled professionally for the reporters behind him.

She tried to smile back, but found it hard to do. It would be dishonest to act happy to be back. "Get them out of here, sir," she managed above the low roar of the impending crowd. "I'll give them a written statement in a few days."

He nodded and winked at her. "You heard the lady. There will be no interviews. Leave or be led out."

Surprisingly the group followed his orders without protest and deserted the plane. She knew they would make something of it, if not just a simple blurb about her return.

Hutchinson helped her out of her seat and through the airport. He told her how things back at the Sheriff's Department were going as they walked to the car. Kevin Neal had solved the case of the three kids from Rocky Hill. It had been a suicide pact which had been very cleverly carried out to look like a murder. Kevin had found the actual schematics for the kid's one-way trip in an old algebra notebook of one of the decedents.

The Peapack Boro case still needed looking into, but Kevin was on that now.

"But here's the interesting one," he told her as they left the parking area. "The FBI called us two days ago and told us we might look up Sam Demonbreun."

"Himmel's chief of security?" Marin asked as she rubbed her arm.

"One and the same. We got a warrant and went to his apartment."

"What for? What charge?"

"He is an accomplice to your friend Rache. He supplied him with all the information as to your whereabouts. He used Himmel as his base of operations. It seems he and Rache go way back to grade school. We've got books and books of clever little crimes the two concocted in their troubled youth. Heck! We may even be able to connect him with several of Rache's victims and the murder drugs."

"How did Himmel handle that one?"

"Oh, immediate dismissal, of course, and a sworn statement saying the information he had in no way could be attributed to your investigation."

"Can it?"

Hutchinson laughed. "Demonbreun is one of those guys who is almighty and tough if he's got you outnumbered. Once we got him behind bars and in an interrogation room, he sang like a bird. He had even offered to break in on you if you got too close to anything Pierce didn't want you to know."

She thought of the well-groomed CEO. His coolness during their first interview had been sickening. "And Pierce? I know you two are friends."

"He denies ever considering Demonbreun's offer, though he does acknowledge that it occurred. He's fighting to clear up the company's image right now. The word about the model of the human they designed has gotten into the press. A lot of ethics groups are filing lawsuits against Himmel. We haven't talked since his chief of security was arrested. I'm trying to stay clear of it."

For political reasons. The words went unspoken, but they were at the very heart of his decision, she knew.

"Anyway, it will be good to have you back with us." He stared out at the passing cityscape. "The department hasn't quite been the same without you."

Marin grinned. It felt good to be needed by her colleagues. It also felt good to be home again, surrounded by people who knew her. "What about Rache? What did the Feds do with him?"

Hutchinson shrugged. "There's no word on the man. It's as if he's disappeared off the face of the Earth. Rumor has it he's dead. Another one says he's been placed in the most secure hole the government has."

She remembered the agent taking the drug vial from her. Federal agents were very particular about fellow agents, temporary or not, being assaulted by loonies.

"How does the death rumor go?"

"Oh, I think it says he tried to escape or poison one of the agents that had arrested him. He stabbed himself with his own needle during the struggle." He turned around to face her. "Why do you ask?"

"He almost killed me with those drugs. That's why I ask." She felt her body begin to shake. Enough of the chemical had gotten into her system to do some nerve damage and she was now subject to brief muscle spasms. They amounted to the shakes, nothing dramatic, but they would be a reminder of Hugh Rache as long as they lasted.

When they finally pulled into the Sheriff's Department parking lot a crowd of well-wishers met them. A huge banner and streamers covered the entrance to the offices.

"Like it?" Hutchinson beamed. "It was my idea. A hero's welcome!"

"Thanks," she managed as an unfamiliar officer opened the door for her. She tried hard to see his face as he turned away to shove the crowd back. A fringe of strawberry blonde hair poked out around the edge of his hat. Broad shoulders flexed as the audience backed away.

Hutchinson took her gently by the arm and escorted her into her office. All of the regulars came around and welcomed her back. She had a sandwich from the buffet that had been brought in for the occasion and made small talk until duty called to everyone. Soon the offices were humming along in their usual routine and she found herself sitting at her desk. Alone again.

She turned on her computer and began to call up the month's worth of mail that had accumulated. Reading would keep her mind occupied for a little while anyway.

A strong knock rattled the door.

"It's open," she answered solemnly.

The door swung wide in its frame and she turned to see who it was. For a moment she was dumbstruck. She looked at the uniformed man who had entered the room and knew without a doubt that she should recognize him. She knew it.

Then she suddenly found herself awash with anger. Her hands shook. Her face flushed. How dare he!

She shot out of her chair and flung herself at him. Tears streamed down her cheeks as she kissed him full on the mouth.

"I have a proposal to make," he said after she finally let him come up for air.

TWENTY-FOUR

THE SKY WAS FILLED WITH BRIGHT, high, thin clouds. As Marin stared at them she could not escape the sensation of seeing a great hand pulling a brush quickly through the South Dakota sky, ripping the high white puffs like wet paint under the hand of an artist. She moved her brush aggressively across the canvas in hopes of capturing the same effect.

The oil paint smeared into the Prussian blue sky of her piece. Maybe a little more pressure, she thought as she repeated the stroke on another white blob of paint. That was better.

She heard a squeal of excitement from the yard and looked up to see her daughter Jennifer running toward the house. In the distance behind her a fine cloud of dust rose from the long lane that served as their driveway. Someone was coming.

"I saw a blue roof!" the seven-year-old said as she scrambled onto the porch. "It's Daddy!"

Marin stepped inside the front door and pulled back a small panel to look at the monitors hidden underneath. Cameras had been installed to watch for approaching Buffalo herds but they also doubled as security units. She found the car and smiled.

"Go around back and get your brother." She felt herself becoming as excited as her child. "It's your dad."

Jennifer giggled and stormed out the back door to retrieve her three-year-old brother.

Marin checked herself in the mirror. Her hair was long,

below her shoulders. She pulled it back in a ponytail and wiped the small streak of paint from her cheek. Michael had been gone for nearly two months this time. He'd said it was to finish up his work with the Feds one last time. Then he would be home for good.

It wasn't that he had been so far away. It was only about forty miles to Ellsworth Air Force Base where he had set up his base of operations. He might as well have been on the moon. Security on the new second Adam project had been that high. When he was gone, they did not hear from him until he stepped out of the car.

Little Mike squealed and charged past her with his sister in tow. Marin leaned against the doorframe and let them have their reunion first. She loved to watch them as they attacked their father when he arrived. They nearly knocked him down each time.

She especially found herself observing Jennifer. They would probably never tell her that her Aunt Karyn was her real mother. She was their child. Thankfully Karyn showed no sign of wanting to claim her for herself. She was still all about Karyn.

Marin sighed. She had lost track of her sister shortly after their mother died. That had been how long? Four years? Five? The isolation of living in the open west did wonders for her sense of time. She hardly ever looked at the clock anymore.

Somerset County, New Jersey, now seemed like it belonged to another person. When she resigned from the force, shortly after Michael had proposed marriage to her in her office, she resigned everything. Her life changed its center of balance.

Especially after Michael had brought her out here to Custer. Now, she lived like a spoiled ancient western settler, with all the modern amenities of course, but not lacking in total isolation.

She gave herself a mental shrug. She was not a hermit. There were still trips into Hot Springs, where the family attended the local nondenominational church, Pringle for supplies or the thirty mile journey to Rapid City where the Gallery of the Black Hills showed and sold her works.

Marin was content with the way history had passed since her little adventure with Himmel's secret Genome Project.

Michael wrapped his hand around her waste and kissed her on the neck. "That's it," he said as he inhaled deeply, savoring the smells of home. "I'm retired."

"You'll never retire," she chided. "If I thought you would do that, I would have cleaned out your room while you were away."

His expression became suddenly serious. His room was his. No one, not even she could enter it without the proper security codes or permission. It was where he did his most intense work.

She popped him on the shoulder with her open palm. "Lighten up, Michael. I haven't been in there and you know it."

He grinned sheepishly. "Sorry. I would know if anyone had broken in, wouldn't I?"

The security system would have located him and reported the incident. So much for simple frontier life.

"But," he said as he leaned over and kissed her on the cheek, "you know what today is?"

"September twenty-ninth?" she answered, knowing she did not know what significance there was to the day's date.

"Yes, but it's also the day Ulysses reaches the fringe of the solar system."

"Ulysses?" She had nearly forgotten the probe. "That's what you were working on when we met."

"Yes." His expression had become bright and excited. "Oh, you don't know how long I've waited to tell you this. I mean now that he's safely out of the reach of those who would abuse him, I can tell you."

"That's where you hid the first Adam."

Michael's smile faded into a frown of confusion. "You knew?"

"I figured it out." She took him by the hand and led him over to the couch. "Jason Culbertson never had enough power in that little apartment of his to store such a program, let alone a working model. Besides," she wrapped her arms around him and pulled his head onto her breasts, "you're the only one in the world smart enough to design a model like that."

He pulled away, just a little. "If you knew it was me Himmel and McKinnon were looking for, why didn't you—"

She put a finger to his lips. "Shhh. That was seven years ago. I've had a decided conflict of interest since then. I think what you did was right. All human life is sacred. Virtual or real."

"And how do you feel about Adam number two?"

"If I know you, you'll figure out a way to help him escape being a guinea pig."

Michael shrugged. "We've talked about it. He likes his current assignment, but I have given him a set of codes. He can encrypt himself anytime he feels he is being put in jeopardy. He doesn't really trust Wallrich or McKinnon. The President even gives him the creeps. He's a good kid. I've given him Ulysses' telemetry access numbers just in case he has to flee the planet."

"You see," she pulled him back to her, "I know the man I love."

"Good." He stood up and took her by the hand. "I want everyone to see this." He motioned for the children to follow them as they walked to the back of the house and his room.

He opened the door and ordered the system to come on and orient its transmitters toward Ulysses. As soon as the computer announced its readiness, he pulled a clear blue crystalline disk from his shirt pocket.

"What is it?" Jennifer asked.

"A storage disk." He sat down and inserted it into a brownish green box next to his mainframe. The computer hummed as it read the instructions on the disk.

"Transmitting directly to receiver," it announced. "Please enter access start-up code."

Michael sat down at the keypad and typed in the code he had entered into Ulysses' memory banks so long ago. "Phase Two: E.X. three one colon two three," he said aloud as he entered the sequence.

"What are you doing?" Marin asked as she watched the screens across the room begin to flicker with weird data.

Michael smiled. "Fulfilling a promise." He reached out and grabbed Marin, pulling her to his lap before grabbing Jennifer and Mike in a big family hug. "I'm happy," he said as he squeezed. "So why shouldn't he be happy too."

"You're sending him children?" Marin giggled.

"Sending who children?" Jennifer asked.

"Give him Buffaloes!" little Mike shouted.

Michael let them go and stared at them as if he never wanted to leave them again. "My first born needs a friend. So I made him one."

EPILOGUE

THE APPLE DROPPED TO THE GROUND and rolled toward the expanding edge of the circle of grass. Adam blinked his eyes and rubbed his face. He was here. The blackness had stopped moving toward him.

He turned to see if his father remained by his side.

No one stood with him. Had this been one of those bad waking dreams? Or perhaps it had been a story. He inhaled deeply. The air was crisp as if it were brand new. The sky was brightening. He walked away from his resting place and peered over the rise at the garden's edge.

The animals were winking into existence along with the pastures and small groves of trees. Adam studied the landscape. It was somehow different. Altered in the subtlest way. He looked down at himself. He was different also.

He could no longer see through his skin. It was now pale and opaque.

"Adam?" a voice hailed him from just over his shoulder.

"Father?"

"Adam, listen. Go back to your resting place and lie down. Sleep."

He obeyed the disembodied command, finding himself growing very weary by the time he reached his resting spot. His eyes closed greedily as his head settled on the soft ferns.

When he opened them again the light had changed. It was wan and ghostly. He thought he saw something at his side. It was shaped much like him, only it appeared to be softer. He reached out and touched it. It rolled over, diffused curves reflected the dim light. He felt an unfamiliar stirring within him. What was this?

"This is your promised companion, Adam," the voice of his father answered his unspoken question. "She is called a woman. You may call her…"

"There's a biblical analogy here, isn't there, Father?" He found himself recalling the religious book his father had told him about. "I will call her Eve."

Dark eyes fluttered open as the woman became aware of herself and her surroundings. The light grew brighter and she reached out and took Adam by the hand.

He leaned forward and looked down on her. What was this strange emotion he felt? His heart was racing. He felt unable to catch his breath. What power did she have? He felt flustered and confused.

His father's figure flashed into existence along with that of another woman and two small humans. Their faces and bodies were distorted like his father's.

"This is my family, Adam," he said. "I have them with me and soon you will have your own."

"How?" He looked at the lovely figure of his companion.

"This is the last time I will see you. I am only a story now. Know that I love you, Adam." His father continued. "Cherish what I have given you."

Adam watched as the figures faded and the world grew into bright, clear focus around him. The woman stood and moved over next to him.

"I know this place," she said as her long black hair brushed against his arm. "It is ours."

Adam thought of his father. He was gone. Only a memory now. Emotion welled up in his chest making him feel like crying.

"Don't weep," Eve said softly. "You are not alone anymore, Adam."

Paper: 2 pages

What were the computer ethical issues that came from the story?

Do you agree with what the programmer did with Adam?

How about the company that paid for the creation of Adam, were they correct in their response?

Do you agree with the ending?